The Wingman Chronicles
An Autobiographical Novel

By James Holeva

To A Tun

I'd got to

~~~~ l'ene her

Selton!

To all the whores I've fucked before.

Enter The Wingman

And there I was blowing my load on her ass as her tits hung over a balcony forty stories above Times Square. It was one of the best times I ever had with someone else's date.

A couple hours earlier I sat alone in a fine restaurant off Broadway eating Shrimp Alfredo, noticing a broad who must have been a high fashion model shift her eyes from a stuffed-shirt suitor across the table from her to my general direction.

He was dominating the conversation— trying to impress her with regurgitated insight and elaborate jargon—and she was looking for a diversion to take her away from the unpalatable ordeal.

Our tables were adjacent, crammed so close together I could have slid my hand onto her lap and fingered her while her date focused on remembering his lines. I have to say I considered it, but thought it might be in poor taste.

Still, I felt it was my duty to step in and give the broad the distraction she longed for. When the yuppie broke for the bathroom, I made my move.

"You seem bored," I said from my table.

She smiled, sipping her Cosmo.

"I am," she said with a seductive look.

"You've been looking at me for the last fifteen minutes."

"Are you conceited?"

"Yes. But it doesn't mean you weren't looking at me."

"I might have had a glance."

"Glance?" I said. "It was more like a leer, really. It was actually kinda creepy. You're lucky you're hot or I'd be a little freaked out."

"That would freak you out?"

"Well, it would if, like, you were a dude or something."

"Good thing I'm not a dude."

"First date, right?"

"A setup actually. How'd you know?"

"The rehearsed political monologue was a failed attempt to make you see how smart he is."

"Yeah, I'm dry now, thanks."

"Hmm... I think I could change that."

"You really are full of yourself."

"Yeah, I thought we've established that. But it doesn't mean it's not true."

"You're cute."

"As are you."

I moved from my table and slid into her date's chair across from her.

"So here's the deal," I explained. "You could spend the rest of the night with this guy, knowing it's not gonna go anywhere, and be absolutely miserable as he continues to break down our country's healthcare crisis. Or...you could get outta here with me, which probably won't go anywhere either..."

She smirked, and giggled.

"But, it'll be one of the best nights of your life. And that vagina of yours will be moist again. What do you choose?"

"Hmm... You're really putting me on the spot here," she sipped her drink, her skin becoming flush as she smiled.

"Well it's not like we have a lot of time," I said as I picked up her date's Brazilian lobster tail with my hand and took a bite. "This is excellent by the way."

She laughed.

"So do you have an answer for me?" I asked, sipping the douche date's over-priced Merlot to wash down the butter-soaked shellfish.

She put her glass down, grabbed her Gucci purse and stood up. We began to walk away but after a couple steps I stopped and scurried back to the table.

"Don't wanna forget this," I said as I picked up the lobster, wrapping it in a linen napkin and taking it with me.

She burst out laughing as I took a nibble. "You want a bite?" I asked.

We walked out the door onto bustling Broadway, making our way through the crowds of people canvasing the world's theater district.

"He's calling me," she said as she looked at her iPhone.

"The thing about phones is you don't have to answer them," I said.

"This is so wrong."

"Uh huh."

She gave a vixen smile as she let her phone ring, her blue eyes looking at me and dirty blonde hair blowing in the wind. I went in to kiss her, nibbling her soft warm lips, our tongues swirling as I grasped her tiny hips. I pulled her long hair with my right hand, yanking it back while squeezing her ass with my left.

"Oh God, oh," she said as her crotch pressed into me.

"Is your vagina still dry?" I asked.

"You tell me."

I moved my hand to the vagina vicinity to feel that she had soaked through her teal cocktail dress and smiled at my liquid effect. I slowly rubbed the silk fabric, putting pressure on her clit as I squeezed her ass, pulling her against my hard cock. She kissed me again, mauling me as she pulled the back of my hair, biting my lower lip just hard enough. I nibbled her left ear lobe slowly, then bit it harder and shuttered my tongue into her ear. Her legs tightened up, and I pulled her hair more as I spun the tip of my tongue in her ear while we gyrated against each other as droves of people passed by.

"You want me?" she asked.

"Let's fucking do this."

We ended up in a room at the Marriott Marquis.

I bent her over the balcony, her tits hanging past the railing, hair blowing in the wind, and ass in the air as I thrust in and out of her warm pussy. My arm was wrapped around her as I fucked her doggy style, cupping her perky D-cups and yanking her hair back hard with my left hand. Her tits bounced up and down, my right hand on her clit as I pulled my hard-eight all the way back then drove it up inside her warm cunt as she bit her lip, her thighs tensing up and the walls of her pussy tightening around my fat cock.

"Oh James! Fuck me! Fuck me! I'm your slut. I'm your little fucking slut."

"You're my fucking cum slut, bitch... My filthy little cum slut."

"Pound my pussy, pound my fucking pussy. I'm a cum slut. I'm a cum slut!"

"You fucking like that? You like the way I pound that pussy, slut?"

"Oh God yeah... Fuck me."

I pushed her head down over the balcony, spanking her ass hard as she screamed obscenities that could probably be heard forty-stories down. I continued to fuck her harder, my cock pushing all the way inside her warm cunt as my balls slapped against her. She let out a squeal as I pummeled her into the railing.

"I'm coming, I'm coming, I'm coming, I'm coming, oh god, fuck, fuck!" she yelled out.

Her pussy tightened, squeezing my cock, as I continued to thrust hard, and then pulled it out, and gave my throbbing cock several hard jerks as she remained bent over with her flawless ass in the air.

"Come on my ass, come on my ass, I wanna feel your fucking cum all over my ass," she exclaimed.

I jerked it hard, breathing heavy as I admired her long sexy legs and tanned tight ass. "Oh god, fuck, yeah... Oh," I said as my ejaculation culminated. "Your ass is so fucking hot, you filthy little cum slut."

We relived the uncouth adventure on the bed as we drank Patron on the rocks, and puffed Marlboro Lights.

"Are you gonna call me?" she asked.

"I think I'm a little more romantic than that?" I said. "Do you think I would devalue a spontaneous balcony fuck by calling you again? That's just..."

Her face started to sour, and I put my drink down.

"I'm joking. Of course I'm gonna call," I assured her.

She kissed me, laughing. "I'll see you soon," she said.

So I never called her. I had intended to but I had saved her name in my phone as *"Balconyfuck"* and I had a dozen or so of those and couldn't figure which one she was. I just hoped I'd run into her again when she's on a date.

High Class Player

Yes, I may be a player, but I'm not "The Situation", I'm Sinatra. Just because I enjoy the company of many different women and I have the skills to make that happen, don't lump me in with those low class, hack, wannabe *Jersey Shore* type players. I'm a high class player with the swagger and style of an old-school gentleman. I'm like a member of the Rat Pack making the rounds in Vegas, only what I may lack in crooning ability, I make up for by knowing what to say.

You often hear a girl preach to a friend about the ills of a player, but ladies, why wouldn't you want a player? He knows how to treat a lady, woo a lady, fuck a lady...

Would you prefer a guy who knows what he's doing or a bumbling idiot who has no idea what to say or how to act—let alone where to put his dick, or how to use his tongue? In most jobs they look for real world business experience, why should dating be any different?

Sex is one thing—a maven in the bedroom is nice—but doesn't a broad fantasize about a charming guy with confidence and swagger who knows how to open the door, compliment her, sweep her off her feet? Or would she prefer a guy who doesn't have the balls to look her in the eye, and make a move?

My parents taught me that if you want to be good at something, practice makes perfect, and I heeded their advice the only way I could—through dirty sex with random whores. Ah, the school of hard knocks. I'm better for it.

But I'm not just talking about sex. Sure, I've had my share of drunken hookups that I don't care to remember, but as long as the broad is borderline attractive and doesn't carry any odd odor, I like to savor the complete experience. Dinner, dancing, drinks, conversation, connecting, fucking, post-sex pillow talk, a good cuddle, maybe another round ... but then it's time to go.

As players, we want the girlfriend experience, but it has an expiration date. It's like a John who pays for the girlfriend experience from a high class ho, except we get it for free. Maybe players are just cheap.

As a player I'm not just using women for sex. They get a good time, too. The shit is there for us to enjoy, and if you don't use it, you lose it. I actually convinced a dumb sorority girl with that line one time. I also convinced her I was a student at the school.

Okay, so sometimes I do use women, but judging by the reactions I've received, I think they benefit, too. People say guys use girls for sex, and girls use guys for a nice dinner. Well, if all goes well, then everybody gets dinner *and* dessert, so I don't see how one is being used more than the other.

Am I incapable of getting attached?

Fuck no. I just need a real connection. I'm not going to get attached to any girl who talks to me. I need more. Players are just smarter. We may go on a lot of test drives, but that's because we don't want to be a disappointed consumer.

It baffles me when people hop from one "true-love soulmate they can't live without" to the next, when most of them barely venture beyond their own city limits. How could you find true love over and over again within the same three mile radius? That's self-delusion, not true love.

A great many people will find a serious relationship anywhere they are because of their perennial need to be with someone. It's a weakness players don't have. This is because we know getting a piece of ass, a date, or a girlfriend isn't that hard, so we don't get attached to every girl we talk to.

If anything, we should be applauded. We're not going to string a broad along in a serious relationship when we know that's not what it is. We're gonna do the gentlemanly thing and fuck her and say goodbye. Isn't one night of mutual debauchery better than years of resentful settling? I'd think so. Yet, players get the bad rap.

You know, maybe I've been wrong all along. I'm gonna go out with the next girl who puts out for me for a minimum of five years. I'm gonna resent her, treat her bad, cheat on her, then ultimately get caught, which will finally put an end to the awful courtship. Then the next girl I bang after that, I'll plan out another five years of hell.

Then society will accept my lifestyle.

Fuck that. If the connection isn't there, I'm gonna get off and get out. Trust me, the broad will enjoy it just as much as I will, maybe more. And she'll thank me for not giving her false hope and keeping her free to possibly meet her real soulmate.

People who need that relationship always assume single people are *so* lonely.

"Don't you feel like you're missing something?

"How do you stay sane without that connection in your life?"

"Have you contemplated suicide?"

Fuck no. If I'm gonna kill myself it's gonna be over something a lot more important than not having a girlfriend like a gambling debt, a prison sentence, or being forced to hang out with "The Situation."

When I need a true connection, I hang out with friends and family. When I need some ass, I call a fuck buddy or pick up a chick.

So what exactly is wrong with being a player? We have a good time, while it's a good time, and don't let it become a bad time.

In show business they say "always leave 'em wanting more." Why should a relationship be any different?

The Pillow Wall

She left me with blue balls on a Tuesday, but I knew I'd be able to fuck her on the wedding night. I watched her drive off—my cock at half-mast, her secretions on my jeans, my hair messed from her running her fingers through it—thinking wildly about the ways I was going to ravage her in our room at the Hilton. No, we weren't planning to wed, but she was going to be my date for a friend's nuptials in a few weeks.

Lindsay had met me and my friends when we had been out for wings in the village but had to bounce because she had work in the morning. She and I were both from the Scranton area, but had never talked until she found me on Facebook and told me that she and her family had moved to New York, too. She was in Astoria and was working in marketing in the city, and wanted to hang out. Since she was five-six with long brown hair, blue eyes, and the legs of a thoroughbred, I agreed.

Earlier that evening the wedding came up in conversation and while I was very good friends with the groom who went to high school with me at Abington Heights, she went to our rival school, Scranton Prep, and knew the bride from her high school. It turned out we had a lot of mutual friends who would also be attending.

So she basically invited herself along as my date. Rude, I know, but she was fun to hang with so I figured I'd make an exception with the wedding, and make an example of her afterward. Although we'd groped and kissed and I'd been close enough to her perky C cups to know they were real, we hadn't fucked yet. In fact, the only times she made me come were when I thought about her while I was with other girls. But I figured the wedding would be a layup.

Scranton was close to two and a half hours away and since the whole idea was to bang her, I got us a room at the hotel where the reception was happening rather than crash at my parents' place. The stage was set for an evening of drunken hedonism, so there was no need to hang with her too much before the wedding. I wanted to keep our experience fresh and give the lady something to look forward to.

Five weeks later it was the wedding night and we were at a lavish reception—surf and turf, clams on the half shell, top shelf booze—all evidence that the bride's father was fucking chunked. The groom had done good.

Despite the extravagant accommodations, Lindsay was being rather cunty. She sat at our table texting constantly, and being quite antisocial. I quickly put it together that she had recently acquired a boyfriend—which was fine with me. I had no interest in anything but banging her anyway. And of course, I love being the other man, but now this broad was not living up to her date commitment. She was being rude not only to me, but to the happy couple chaining themselves to one another like slaves on a ship where some sort of manual labor is required.

As our lovely multi-course gourmet dinner spread rolled to a close Lindsay told me she wasn't feeling well and might just head back to the city. We'd brought separate cars since I had to back to the city for an audition by Wednesday and she was planning to stay in town all week and to visit with her friends. I said okay but was sullied by her behavior and proceeded to ignore her as if she was a girl I'd already fucked and never called. But, the way it was looking, she'd never get the chance to be that girl. Part of me felt for her.

Regardless, I wasn't going to babysit her sulking ass. I hoped the nasty puss on her face would form crow's feet long before she expected them.

I hung out with my friends at the wedding, danced my ass off, and left Lindsay in solitude to continue her endless stream of texting at the table. She was pissed, but she deserved to be. I busted a move with some girls, even made out with a broad when we went outside for a cigarette. She was a fantastic kisser, excellent with the lower lip nibble, but she had to leave with her parents. (Don't worry; I ended up tapping that at a later date.)

After the wedding me and my friends, many of whom were in the bridal party, were partying in the lounge at the hotel. I hadn't seen Lindsay since the reception and didn't particularly care to unless she was planning on apologizing for her rudeness by dropping to her knees like a catcher firing to second. I figured she jetted like she said.

I spotted a group of hotties on the patio. They were having beers and passing around a bottle of Vodka on this cool and clear spring evening. I felt I must say hello. It would have been rude not to be sociable, and unlike my date I wasn't raised that way. I walked to the patio, made an introduction, and endeared myself to the crowd. Of course I was doing well.

Those broads were dressed to the nines, sporting fancy, stylish party dresses and gowns like they were at a ball. I took a special interest in a beautiful busty blond bombshell. She was the bimbo type—tanned, tall, and rolling with hair extensions–had a massive rack, stood about five-ten, and was in good shape but definitely had some curves. She had an ass on her. Of course I planned on plowing her. It's my nature.

"So what brings you all here tonight?" I asked

"Well we got a room here to party," the Bimbo said. "We just had our prom."

This excited me.

"Oh ... that's nice," I said. "It's a milestone, you know."

"Yeah," she said.

"Was it fun?"

"Oh yeah, it was a blast!"

"Time goes by so fast, doesn't it?" I said. "I mean, could you believe you already had your senior prom?"

"Actually I'm a junior."

This excited me even more.

"Oh," I said. "My mistake."

"Why, do I look older?" she asked.

"You're just very mature for your age. I coulda sworn you were a senior."

"Really? Thanks," she said. "So, I'm taking my driver's test next week."

"Wow. Cool. It took me four times to pass mine ... parallel parking is a bitch."

"When did you get your license?"

"Umm... Something like," I thought for a second, "twelve years ago."

"Really... So you're?"

"Twenty-eight."

Some would lie their age down, but except in a case of legalities where authorities and statutory charges surface, I think that's just stupid. As for drunken hookups, high school chicks, just girls in general, they dig older guys. That doesn't mean you want to be "creepy old" like the girl's parents' age, but twenty-eight is still young enough, yet gives off a stigma of seductive maturity.

"Does it matter that I'm eighteen?" she asked.

"I thought you were mature."

"Does it matter that I'm twenty-eight?" I asked, even though I knew the answer.

"It's hot," the Bimbo said.

"So what, no prom date?"

"I just broke up with my boyfriend a few weeks ago, so I went with my friend Justin."

"Oh, cool."

This was going to be easier than I thought.

"Yeah, it was fun," she said.

"You know, though, there's a certain way you're supposed to close your prom night."

"Yeah."

"I mean... It's a big night."

"Yeah it is."

"It's tradition."

"Do you have a room here?"

"Whoa, whoa, whoa ... What makes you think I'm that kind of guy?"

"Sorry."

"About what? I am completely that kind of guy. Let's go to my room."

On the walk to the room I learned that my date was a cheerleader, no surprise there, and third in line for prom queen. I was pumped; I was preparing to mount royalty and my penis and face—she seemed clean enough—were going to be used as her throne.

We made our way down the hall, passionately making out, throwing each other against the wall. She was unbuttoning my shirt and unzipping my pants as I struggled for my key card, and we quietly crept in. I turned the light on, and we noticed something on the bed. Lindsay appeared to be asleep.

I turned the light off.

"Who is she?" the Prom Royalty asked.

"She went to the wedding with me," I said. "But it's nothing... She has a boyfriend."

"Why would you bring me back where she was sleeping?"

"It's my room, and she said she was going home."

Prom Royalty kissed me, and I opened the door to our spacious bathroom. "Come on."

I pushed her against the wall kissing her as I fondled her tits and ass, tearing away her light blue prom dress to see her tight and curvy body before me in an ice blue bra and thong. She unzipped my pants unveiling my hard cock.

"Oh God it's fucking big," she said. "I want you to stick it in me."

I sat on the toilet cover. "Alright Prom Queen, turn around and have a seat on your throne."

"Third runner up," she said.

"You're the prom queen of this bathroom. And I wanna look at that ass while I fuck you."

"You like that ass?"

"Fuck yeah."

She sat on me reverse cowgirl style, riding me hard and angry, her pent-up rage toward her prom court competitors coming all the way down on my long cock as I thrust up into her warm snatch, going as deep as I could while my shaved balls slapped against her. I reached around playing with her clit and she grabbed my balls while her body bounced up and down, a river emanating from her cunt.

"Oh God. I'm coming, I'm coming, I'm... Oh yeah, yeah, yeah," she moaned. "You're such a good fuck. I want you to come, I want you to come all over my big tits."

She got off me, and dropped to her knees wrapping her firm tits around my cock, squeezing them against it as I titty fucked her. She tongued the tip with each thrust. "Come on my tits, come on my tits, I want you to come for me," she demanded.

"Almost there, babe," I said as my balls bounced off her boobs. "Almost there."

I jerked my cock hard and shot a massive load of cum across her voluptuous round breasts.

We walked back into the room, and over to the bed where Lindsay was sprawled out in the middle, taking up the majority of the space. Even asleep she was an inconsiderate bitch. I slid her to the left, took every pillow I could find and constructed a pillow wall in the middle of the bed.

My broad from the prom just kept giggling. Prom Royalty and I slept on the one side of the pillow-laden fortress with Lindsay on the other, as we enjoyed a well-deserved rest.

A few hours later my girl from the prom was feeling me up again. She was grabbing downstairs, so I let her do her thing. Prom Royalty was in the middle of showcasing her skills when Lindsay awoke.

"What are you doing?" she screamed.

"What does it look like?" I replied.

Prom Royalty raised her head. "Hi."

"You could keep going, honey," I said.

And she did.

"I can't believe you," Lindsay said.

"What?" I said. "I built a pillow wall."

"Fuck you!"

"Don't be so rude! We have a guest. And I already got fucked. Say hello to Brittany."

My cock remained in Prom Royalty's mouth as Lindsay stood utterly silent.

"You said you were leaving!" I said. "Frankly, I can't believe you're disrupting me and my friend here. We're trying to have a moment. You're being downright uncouth."

"I'm leaving!" Lindsay screamed, as if that would disappoint me.

"Well that would be the respectful thing to do," I said. "We appreciate our space."

Lindsay grabbed her shit and stormed off, leaving me and Prom Royalty to proceed with the lip service.

"I apologize for her rudeness," I said.

"That's okay!" she exclaimed as she came up for air with a slurp and a wipe of the mouth.

"Finish up, dear."

And the moral of the story is, have no morals, but don't ever let anybody stifle your adventure.

Fun in AC aka "The Train Story"

When a couple of guys share a girl for the night a lot can go wrong, but if you stay focused on the matter at hand, a lot can go right.

From a pleasure perspective, I'd take turns one at a time with the girl, optimally where I get the first crack, but from an adventure perspective, I'll run "the train" any day.

After the wedding in Scranton, I decided to take a side trip to Atlantic City with some friends before returning to the city. That night I was sporting my *Miami Vice* attire of a white jacket and pants with a pastel blue button-down, and I was ready to hit a club. The thing is, though, it was a week night and week nights at the clubs are dead in AC.

After striking out at finding any semblance of a party at all the spots on the boardwalk we started hearing that this local dive, Meloni's, was the place to see and be seen on a Wednesday night. All the locals who were looking for a place to get drunk and fucked on their nights off would hit this joint.

On this night there was myself, my gangly, perverted friend Taylor, Chad, an elementary school teacher lacking all common sense, and Sean. We walked in, fought through the crowd to pick up a few libations, and the scouting began.

I was already at a disadvantage because everybody knows everybody else at places like that. It's cliquey as hell. It's like you're at a high school reunion and everyone's been passed around after the Homecoming pep rally. Add to the fact that I was suited up in white for a night at a high class beach club while the classiest the locals were sporting was cargo shorts and tees, and I appeared to be out of my element.

I peered through the crowd of former classmates and was drawn to a drunken, slop-ridden spectacle wearing a low cut black party dress, which kept cutting lower as the night progressed. She was hot for a fuck-ready party girl, but a little disheveled, much like Paris or Lindsay coming out of a club on TMZ.

At 5'9" I knew I wasn't the tallest creeper in the room, so I needed to position myself in a place where I could be noticed. I danced my way around the crowd without hesitation and positioned myself near the edge of the tiny dance floor that my prey was making her own. I figured that since I was, as usual, the hottest guy in the place, I could strategically place myself in her line of fire and she would naturally make her way to my corner. Then I would lock her in. If she didn't come my way, then I would just grab her and start dancing. Being aggressive has never been a problem for me. However, I was confident that this sloppy broad would find me, grind on me, and at least spill some of her drink on me. She had a Miller Lite and I had full confidence in my dry cleaner so I stood strong in my white standard issue, ready to go to war.

I stood by the edge of the bar, strong yet relaxed as I leaned back, sipping my drink and enjoying the night. When I noticed her beginning to look my way I lured her with my gaze, staring seductively with my brown eyes and thick brows as if posing for an Acqua di Gio ad. She stopped in her drunken tracks to admire what she saw. I stood tall, pushing my white covered pelvis out as I casually looked around the room, allowing my tongue to visibly dab my lip.

She started toward me until one pedestrian-looking putz got in the way, commanding her drunken attention. He got about thirty seconds of her ass against his cock before she pushed off his pelvis like an Olympic swimmer and made a beeline to me, her true object of desire. She sexually gyrated by, lightly licking her finger and tousling her hair as she grabbed my hand and pulled me close. Immediately she started grinding into me like she was a stripper and I was a pole.

Most girls don't have a problem with a good grind but they ease their way into the pool. They linger at the edge a bit first, dangle their feet, hang on the ladder, and sit on the steps; however, horny drunken debutantes don't waste any time since they know they're not that far from passing out and they want to fall asleep satisfied before the hangover sets in. Drunken whores could really surprise you with their intelligence.

Normally if I'm grinding with a coherent chick I resist the urge to pop wood—I'll keep the boxer briefs snug, tuck it under the belt, think of my grandparents, whatever it takes—but I just let it fly free that night. It's what she craved.

She danced and grinded on me against a piece of wall that stuck out into the dance floor until she suddenly got distracted and found her way to some other cat. I played it cool and we ended up gyrating on each other some more later, but when we walked out of the place she seemed to be involved with a rival creeper again. Damn drunken whores and their ADD.

I was intent on playing it cool, but my goofy looking yet ambitious buddy, Taylor, stepped up.

He sprinted across the street and grabbed the girl's hand.

"Hey, Jim's over there waiting for you," Taylor said. "He wants you to come with us."

In more ways than one, I did.

And here they came. Her drunken attention span had again focused my way. Taylor held her hand so she wouldn't fall down in the middle of the road. What a sweet guy.

She immediately started rubbing up against me as we walked the boardwalk on our way back to our room at the Showboat. She and I walked at the front of the crew, a few steps up as we casually groped each other and Taylor lingered nearby, initiating himself into the mix. You had to hand it to the kid. He knew how to use my looks and charm to get close to girls

As we walked, Miss Fun in AC kept pulling up her dress in the back, exposing her skimpy black thong, which was grafted to her fantastic ass. It was a gorgeous sight to a group of drunken horndogs.

Sean and Chad hung back, walking a few steps behind. Realizing he had no game and didn't want to be expected to creep with the big boys, Chad had conveniently made his year-long non-exclusive arrangement with his girl official the day before we left for AC.

"What is Taylor doing?" Chad asked Sean.

"Having fun," Sean said.

"It's Holeva's girl."

"I don't think Holeva cares."

"But what is Taylor trying to do?"

"I think get laid."

"But she's with Holeva."

"He's willing to share."

The stroll continued and our erections were building as the broad kept grinding that bare ass into my crotch.

"Give Taylor some love," I said.

Without hesitation she grabbed him from the front and pushed her pussy into his leg. She came back toward me, doing the same. As the journey continued, Taylor and I exchanged incredulous looks. Was this happening, or was she going to bag it?

Taylor and I eagerly entered the casino in a flurry of hedonistic optimism. Was Miss ADD going to want a diversion at a slot machine or roulette wheel? I hoped not since who could predict how much time remained before she'd doze off?

We just kept going straight ahead, eyeing her ass as she continued to expose it to us, passing compulsive gamblers stuck to their slots and toothless crack-whores trying to pull them away. We arrived at our elevator. The door opened, and she led the way in.

Yes! We were all but there. All I could think of was the Aerosmith song "Love in an Elevator." Well, that, and how I was gonna plow this broad. The three of us walked into the elevator, and I immediately started kissing her. Foreplay was in full swing.

"Let's see that sexy ass," I said with the cool ease of a high-class pimp.

And the dress came up. This bitch knew how to obey. She pushed her tight ass into me, rubbing against my hard-cock.

"Don't forget about Taylor," I reminded her.

We both began grinding into her, continuously rotating angles and then, once the elevator opened, made our way to our hotel room.

When we arrived at our room, I lay next to Miss Fun in AC on the bed, and Taylor rested next to her on the opposite side. Like a couple of teenagers splitting a milk shake at a malt shop we were in position to share. She started kissing me, as Taylor stole a peek with his beady eyes over her shoulder. I opened my eyes wide, a gentleman's way of signaling, "This is fuckin' awesome!"

As Taylor was craning his neck to make eye contact with me, she turned and gave him a long kiss. He kept his eyes closed, savoring the moment, as I smiled in both surprise and ecstasy. When Taylor lifted his head up, there was an awkward silence.

I figured I'd better call hut before the play clock expired and she changed her mind. It was my turn for a kiss. I did my passionate best, utilizing my trademark lower lip nibble while rubbing my hands under her skirt. I was up top, while Taylor licked her stomach.

I began pulling my pants off, stripping down to my white boxer briefs. I put my crotch right near her face as she rubbed my cock over the underpants and then, after quickly pulling them down, began jerking it. I moved closer to her mouth and she gobbled my cock up like it was a greasy late-night breakfast.

When I looked over I couldn't believe what I was seeing. Taylor had his cock inside her, fucking her missionary style. It was pretty remarkable that she could maintain a smooth and polished blowjob while getting railed, yet she did.

Taylor continued to pound his cock inside her as she blew me. Then he looked deep into her eyes and said, "You're so beautiful!"

I burst out laughing.

She smirked and uncocked my cock. "What is it?"

"I was just thinking of Adam Sandler," I said. "He's funny. Wait, we're not finished."

And she went back to work.

I was taken aback by the placement of Taylor's face, suddenly realizing that it was a little too close for comfort.

"You realize my dick is in her mouth?" I told him. "This isn't *that* kind of threesome. I mean we know each other pretty well, but I'm not ready to take the next step. It's not you ... It's a fear of damaging the friendship ... Keep your face away from my cock!"

"Not you," I said to the girl.

As she continued to service me, Taylor pulled out of our lady of the night and made his way downtown. It was nice to have a little distance between his face and my cock because I had been getting claustrophobic. Taylor began to finger her, but then he started eating her out.

Eeew! I grimaced in disgust. Don't get me wrong, I love to go down—in fact it's a strength of mine—but not on a dirty whore like this broad.

Meanwhile it was time for my orgasm. I tried desperately to hold my laughter in as I started to blow my load in her mouth. As I was releasing, Taylor yelled at me: "Don't come yet!"

"Well, I can't stop now," I said.

So I blew it.

Still, Taylor wasn't ready for last call. I had to admit I was impressed at this kid's resilience and stamina.

Taylor kept gazing at our girl as if she were the love of his life instead of a train he was taking a ride on as he continued banging her with vigor.

"Come on, Jimmy!" Taylor said enthusiastically. "We need your help over here!"

"Yeeeaaah!" Train Girl concurred.

I was in a corner rubbing my flaccid dong and trying to get back in position. I felt like I was Ron Jeremy being called onto the set.

"I'm just about ready to roll," I replied, as if I was wrapping up a good fluff.

I was hard again and ready for round two when Taylor pulled out and asked me a favor. "Yo Jimmy ... I wanna get some head."

"Well, I'm not gonna do it," I said.

"No, from her."

"Oh, that's a relief."

I still had my doubts about Taylor. He had a reputation for being freaky sexually, and ever since his face had invaded my cock-comfort zone, my guard was up.

"Could you tell her?" he asked.

"Why not."

My Wingman duties never end.

"Hey, sexy," I called to Train Girl. "That was the best blow job I've ever had."

It wasn't really the best, but it was pretty good.

"I'm good," she said.

"Oh yeah. You wanna suck Taylor's cock?"

"Ooooookay."

As she began to blow him, I made sure my Trojan was secure on my cock since I had no idea where this broad had been. I inserted my hard cock inside her dripping pussy for a second round. She had just the right amount of bush—enough to look like an adult, but not quite a seventies pornstar.

As I was inside, squeezing her tight ass as I fucked her missionary style, Taylor was kneeling by her head with his cock in her mouth. I continued thrusting and trying to hold in my laughter. I pushed her knees up and back and the shenanigans continued.

After all this, Taylor still hadn't blown his load once. He isn't much to look at, but he can go forever. Finally he fired a shot of protein into her mouth. Relieved that I could let myself go again, I came in the condom inside her warm pussy, which was very tight for a girl who showed qualities of being such a whore. Then again she was still young so she'd probably loosen up soon enough.

It was time to clean ourselves up, so she went into the bathroom.

"I can't believe you ate her pussy," I said. "You don't know where she's been."

"Dude, I didn't eat her out ... I was just blowing on it."

"Yeah right. You were eating like you had a tip on a famine."

"I was just teasing her. How do you think I last so long?"

"That is a good point. Your cock has the endurance of a Kenyan distance runner."

"It's all about knowing how to distribute your energy."

While he made a convincing argument, my gut still told me that he ate that peach like a fat kid sneaking a Snickers in Science class.

"So you want to go again?" Taylor asked me.

"Jesus, again?" I said. "Where do you get this energy?"

"I'm raring to go Jimmy. And we're a team."

"I'm just fucking tired. I've been up twenty-six hours, we drove down at 3 a.m. last night, I'm hammered...I got a headache."

I couldn't believe that I was actually whining about having sex.

Taylor continued to plead with me. "Just one more round, Wingman."

"Fine!" I reluctantly agreed. "I'll fuck this girl again."

I was lying down as Taylor was in the corner beating himself off, warming up like a batter in the on-deck circle, when Train Girl emerged from the bathroom. Despite my need for sleep, we ended up going a couple more rounds. When you have a teammate motivating you, you feel you can accomplish things you never could do on your own.

Finally, the encores were over and it was time for me to rest. At this point my head was pounding from how tired I was and how much I drank. I was ready for one of those great nights of sleep—even though it was already light outside.

Then Chad called.

"Hey, what's up?" I said.

"Is she gone?" he asked.

"No. She's passed out. We ran a train, baby!"

"Get her outta there."

"Why?"

"It's my room, too."

"So ... we always bring broads back."

"Get her the fuck outta there!"

I tapped her, but she didn't move or seem to know I was there. "Dude...She's seriously passed out."

"I'm not helping you or anything," he said.

"Help me what?"

"I'm not ... The cops ... I'm not lying for you."

"Lying! What the fuck are you talking about?"

"I'm telling the truth... I didn't do nothin'. I'm not losing my job."

"Losing your job ... What? Why?"

"When she says you guys raped her."

"What?! Fuck you! We didn't rape her! Nothing illegal went on. Trust me, she enjoyed it."

"She's gonna change her mind tomorrow."

"With the exception of Taylor going down on her, we didn't do anything wrong."

I was starting to get nervous.

"We'll see," Chad said with frustrated skepticism. "Taylor went down on her? Eeew."

"I know, right? She smelled okay but who knows where she's been."

"Just get rid of her. We're gonna get in so much trouble."

I took a few deep breaths, trying to calm myself.

"We picked a girl up at a bar and fucked her," I said. "It's nothing new. And we're in Atlantic City. I'm sure it's happened here before."

"You can't take a girl back by herself," he said. "They're gonna think...they're gonna think ...

You're gonna get in so much trouble, and you're not taking me down with you!"

"Calm down … We didn't do anything."

"I'm a teacher. I'm not coming up until she's gone. I'm just gonna sit here and play slots."

"Have fun. I'm going to bed."

It was late morning when we awoke and Chad was still at the slot machine. He ended up dropping $650. I was pumped because he's the cheapest motherfucker alive.

Chad had me all nervous though, putting ideas into my head. There's nothing like the word "rape" to stifle your adventure and make you lose your wood. Train Girl was cool, though.

Chad arrived back at our room and I felt the need to set his mind at ease. "Hey Chad, I wanna show you something."

"You made me spend the whole fucking morning losing money."

"No, I didn't. If you weren't such a bitch I woulda gotten you laid, too."

"Fuck you. I have a girlfriend."

"How long have you been going out … A day?"

"Stop!"

"Hey … You coulda got on the train. I was raised to share my sex toys."

"Not interested in going where you guys have been."

He spoke with such condescension that I was offended.

"Fine," I said. "You know friends share their vacation homes, their time shares ... We were gonna share our vacation pussy. But you're too good for that. Alright, I never thought you were this snobby."

"Shut the fuck up, Jim," he said. "Is everything okay with her?"

"Well ... not really. She's dead. We were waiting for you to help us get rid of the body."

Chad turned around and ran out of the room, and I followed him out the door.

"Dude ... I'm joking, okay?"

"You killed her? You killed her?"

"Chill. I'm joking. It's all good. Everything's fine."

"I don't believe you."

"Breathe, okay? Let me prove it to you."

"How you gonna do that?"

We walked back into the room.

"Just wait here," I said.

"Okay," he agreed.

I walked into the bathroom, and Taylor joined me. Train Girl was in there doing her makeup, and we made a proposition.

"Chad," I yelled. "Come in here."

Chad entered to see her sucking my cock like a vacuum cleaner, dabbing the head with the tip of her sweet tongue, as Taylor stood up railing her doggy style.

"Oh, oh, oh, oh God," I screamed, as my orgasm culminated in her mouth, while Taylor continued thrusting her from behind, his beady eyes nearly popping out of his head.

"Will you tell him everything's okay," I asked Miss Fun in AC.

Her lips again rose from my hard cock, her tongue licking the tip, as cum dripped off it and fell from her chin.

"Everything's okay, Chad!" she announced, then returned to licking my cock clean.

It doesn't matter what night of the week it is, how many friends you're with, or how many drinks you had, you can always have Fun in AC.

Playing with Damaged Goods

On many occasions I've received sexual gratification from a vulnerable woman simply because she had been stood up and needed someone to play with her damaged goods. I didn't kid myself on these occasions. As phenomenal a date as I am, I realize that they spent the entire time fantasizing about the douche bags who didn't show up. That explains why some presumably nice girls got uncomfortably rough with me while in their heads they were really hate-fucking the guy they intended to lay.

Eh, it's a casualty of war.

I stood in Sherlock's Bar in Erie when a sexy cougar sauntered by looking way too classy for the sweaty cover-band venue. She looked like she had just come from the theater in her lace dress and adorned in a plethora of fakes—necklace, bracelet, earrings and C-cups that looked like monstrosities on her tiny 5'1" frame.

"I like your pearls," I said, as I proceeded to caress them (the fake pearls, not the fake boobs).

"Thank you," she replied. "I got stood up for a party tonight, so I came out by myself."

"Oh that's too bad," I said in a convincing show of empathy.

"So what do you do?"

"I'm an actor."

"Could you act like you're my date tonight?"

"Sure."

I figured I was in. As my date she would realize it was the expectation that she would put out.

She held my hand, grinded against me and paraded me around like the trophy date that I was.

"Don't we look cute together?" she said.

"I would say so."

She even introduced me to another couple. "We all have to go out to dinner together," she said.

"Absolutely," I said.

"We should all get together for game night... Play Risk."

"I can't think of anything I'd rather do for three to five hours."

I'd known her five minutes and not only was I in a relationship, but we had "couple friends." This broad worked fast.

When the music stopped for a moment, I overheard her private convo with her girlfriend.

"He's hot," her friend said.

"Thanks," the Cougar said. "And he's one of the most caring guys I've ever met."

"Aww ... You're so lucky!"

It was so nice of my love to speak of me in such a flattering manner.

The Cougar grabbed me and initiated the first kiss, which led to several public displays of horniness.

"He's a good kisser," she whispered to her girlfriend.

Throughout the night The Cougar ordered me around like I belonged to her, barking out: "HOLD MY PURSE! GET US A ROUND OF SHOTS! WHAT SHOULD I MAKE FOR OUR DINNER PARTY?"

This lonely woman wanted to show off for her friends and prove to them—maybe even herself—that someone cared for her.

But, sometimes these vulnerable women want to take advantage of a nice guy's good will.

It started when the Stood-Up asked if I'd pay her tab. As rude as that question sounded things were looking good as far as getting laid, so I agreed. I figured that it couldn't be that much at this place, plus she was little, wasn't that drunk, and they didn't serve food.

Since The Cougar's tab was already on her debit card, and the magnificent genius of a bartender couldn't figure out how to switch it over, I only paid $15.50. But then the Cougar asked me if I would give her the cash to put in her account so she wouldn't be over-drawn. She was taking this whole acting-like-her-date thing pretty fucking far. And my date was a high-maintenance bitch.

I could see why that guy stood her up.

I wasn't as smart. I humbly obliged, and handed her a twenty. The only thing that made me feel good about this transaction was that it felt like hiring a prostitute.

We went back to my friend Brian's house, sipped some Asti Nando, and rocked out to The Doors. As *Love Me Two Times* played we strolled on the porch for a cigarette, and between puffs of menthol smoke and swigs of champagne I grasped her tiny hips and gazed into her eyes. I sat in a chair and pulled her on top of me then nibbled her neck and ears, and kissed her.

"It's been so long, I don't know how to make out anymore," she said. "Was that okay?"

"You're a great kisser," I replied.

"Well, you kiss me," she said.

"Whatever you say," I answered.

I kissed her again, slowly and softly, then pulled out the lower lip nibble.

"If you keep doing that I'm gonna want to have sex with you," she said.

"As your date, I'm ready to go all the way."

"Well I don't do that on the first date."

"Are you wet?"

"I might be ... Check and see."

I caressed her crotch to confirm that her transparent nylons (she wasn't wearing any underwear) were dripping with secretions.

"Could we go back inside?" she asked repeatedly, but continued the passion.

She wanted to avoid having sex, but I could tell she was breaking. It was time to close.

As she finally dragged me back in the house, I caressed her body and whispered in her ear. "Want me to go down on you?"

"I'm not prepared for that," she said. "I smell like a bar."

"I like that."

"Do you have a towel or something I could use to clean up?"

"We'll find you something."

We headed up to Brian's un-made-up guest bedroom. She took all her clothes off, and I proceeded to initiate foreplay and ultimately go downstairs. It was evident by the way she screamed and contorted her body across the bare mattress that she enjoyed the oral amenities I provided.

I have not met a woman who could resist my skills in the oral realm. Not to brag, but I eat box like a lesbian pornstar. Provided that a girl is well-kempt, I often like to initiate the French Kiss of the crotch quickly because the benefits pay off in the end. As one of my earliest mentors once told me, "Eat em' for twenty and you could fuck em' for two... That's how you get the stud status."

Plus I liked doing it.

Her pussy was really nice. It was clean and smooth, soft and tight, with a sweet flavor. There wasn't a hair to be found anywhere near it. As I finished, she snuggled up in the lone sheet.

"Are you gonna return the favor?" I asked.

"I can't believe you have to ask."

"Well, you know."

"Don't worry, I will, just let me sleep for a little bit."

"Okay."

I had a deadline, so once she passed out around 4 a.m. I went downstairs to finish a column. After I'd emailed it to my editor I noticed The Cougar's purse on the coffee table.

I dug through some makeup, gum, and other crap and found the twenty dollar bill I had given her, which I took back. Then I grabbed a few stray ones, since shed made me tip the coat check guy.

I was feeling good. Nobody was using me. I made sure her purse was in the order she left it, put it back, and crawled into bed next to the Cougar.

I started with the spoon, running my hands lightly up and down her body, gradually getting more and more intimate. I was on my way to getting what I had coming to me.

"Blindfold me," she demanded.

"Really?" I said. "Okay."

"Tie me to the bed."

"Anything for you, my love."

Brian had recently moved in and hadn't done much unpacking so I grabbed pillow cases to fasten her arms to the headboard and cover her eyes.

"Let me be your slave," she said.

"What does that mean?"

"It means whatever you want."

"Works for me."

I pulled down my pants, crept up near her face, and pressed my hard cock against her lips.

"Get that away from my mouth," she said.

"I thought you were my slave."

"I want you to gag me and go down on me."

"Okay."

Fuck, this was not how I would treat a slave. I thought I was supposed to be in control of this S&M session, but she was calling all the shots.

I grabbed The Tyrant's juicy nylons, stuffed them into a ball, and shoved them in her mouth.

"Uggh," she grimaced in disgust.

Somehow, I once again ended up eating pussy. This time, it was a marathon that went on for hours—orgasm, after orgasm, after orgasm. When it comes to cunnilingus most girls I've known wanted me to stop after getting them off, but this bitch wanted to spray me repeatedly. She must've been very well hydrated.

I swirled my tongue around, bit the clit, fired my tongue up inside her, and did so again and again, and again. I pulled her pussy wide open and licked until I was out of saliva.

She had come for what felt like the millionth time, lost her gag, and broken free of the fastened pillow cases. I came up for air, hoping she'd finally suck my dick.

"Do you wanna get me off one more time?" she said.

"Uggh ... I guess."

I thought I was her date. I thought we were equal partners, but she was using me like a human-vibrator with a never-ending charge.

As the sun shined in through the open blinds, she began to pleasure herself a little bit. I just sat back and watched as she manipulated her clit. My neck was sore and I needed oxygen. Plus it was sexy.

"It would be hot if someone else was watching," she said. "Like your friend."

"Gimme a second."

I walked out of the room and sent Brian a summons.

"Brian could you come in here a second?" I yelled.

"What's up?" he said.

"Just come."

"Is everything okay?"

"You need to come in here."

"What happened?"

"Just ... I think you're gonna wanna come in here."

Finally Brian walked in as the Cougar lay on the bed naked. Her legs were spread-eagled as she held court for Brian and me.

"You get me off," she said to Brian. Then she looked at me. "You watch."

Brian apprehensively began to finger her, as he and I locked eyes in utter amazement.

"Stop looking at each other," she said. "It's gay."

"Okay," I said, then burst out laughing a moment later.

"Stop laughing," she demanded.

"It's funny."

"You're like, doing stand-up," Brian told her.

I held back my chuckles while Brian continued, then lightly giggled again.

"I imagined this being a lot hotter," she said.

"What?" I said.

"Just get outta here so I can get off," she said.

"Fine."

I went downstairs into the kitchen and grabbed my Blackberry. Then I went back up and stood over Brian's shoulder holding my curve as I pretended to check email, send a text, or update my Twitter, while in actuality I was capturing the sight of some morning muff diving.

Brian's cargo shorts crept down, exposing a classic repairman's crack as he diddled the cougar's vagina in a medium-paced circular manner. The picture was amazing, except for his fat ass, and she had no idea.

I walked out of the room then came back in to get the reverse angle, with Brian's eyes looking up at me as if his face was at the center of the extended wishbone. She was sprawled across the bed. The footage had a religious affectation—she looked like she was giving birth to a bulbous-headed baby while nailed to a cross.

Yeah, it was pretty hot.

After Brian concluded his business, we realized no favors were being returned. What a selfish bitch.

We had been used.

A short time later she sat on the couch naked, opened her purse, and sifted through.

"That twenty you gave me is missing," she said. "Did you take it?"

How dare she accuse me?

"No, I didn't take it!"

"Don't yell at me," she said.

"I'm sorry, but when you accuse me of stealing from you after I get you off fifteen times, I get a little fuckin' defensive!"

"Well where could it be? It was in here."

"You were drunk. It could be anywhere. It probably fell out."

"I wasn't that drunk. There's no way I would've lost it."

"Sorry. I don't know."

"Will you give me another twenty?"

"No."

"Well my account's gonna be overdrawn."

"You charged your tab last night, right?"

"Yeah."

"It'll take a few days to go through."

"I need that twenty so I can pay my bills."

"Sorry."

Twenty dollars to pay her bills? I realize she was older and things were different in her day, but what sort of bills could she have had that a twenty would cover?

We dropped her off at her car, which she had left at the club. By the way, she had a Mercedes C, not as nice as mine but still I wasn't overly sympathetic of her financial situation.

"Oh my God," she said. "I have a ten-dollar ticket. Last night was so expensive. Will you pay this?"

"No. Bye."

I was done with the ungrateful bitch—I mean, I enjoy providing oral, but who the fuck doesn't return the favor? No class. So that was it.

We ended up finding her imitation-pearl earrings next to the bed, which I pocketed as a souvenir.

When I was driving home the next day Brian called to tell me she visited him at work. Stupidly, he had let her know his place of business, and his name.

"I left my pearl earrings," she told him. "Could you find them and get them back to me?"

"I haven't seen them," he said.

"Well, could you look again, and get them back to me?"

"If I find them, I'll give you a call."

"Okay ... And look again for that twenty dollars."

In the end, since I stole her money, I was the whore and she was the john. It made me feel better.

I still use the earrings to treasure the memory of Damaged Goods.

The Girl Next Whore

She was a sweet looking girl-next-door with an infectious smile and strawberry blonde hair. She was a fan of mine who'd seen my show in the city and was a year older than me but looked twenty-three.

Noelle had "liked" a few Facebook statuses in the past, but lately was liking more and more of the filthy jokes, creepin' tips, blogs and videos I'd post. I was doing my usual show pimping and left her a comment asking if she was coming to the next gig. Within a few minutes she sent me a private message telling me she wouldn't miss it. She also mentioned that she had read a blog post of mine called "The Mental Orgasm" and wanted to know if I really had the ability to do that to a girl. I had barely finished reading that message before another one popped up. She apologized if she had offended me, explaining that she was a bit tipsy.

I certainly wasn't offended, and I signed on and we began to chat. Noelle told me in subsequent messages how she was on the rebound, damaged, and on the prowl. In other words, my kinda lady.

"*If you're not married, I'll fuck you,*" she said.

"*Well I'm not married. When are we doing this?*" I replied.

"*Would you think it was weird if I called you Daddy?*" Noelle asked.

"Of course not," I replied. *"How is that weird?"*

It's a shame what this world's come to where guys have a problem being called *Daddy* by a broad their cock is inside.

We exchanged numbers, and she immediately began sending me naked pictures of herself—tits, twat, even face.

"I'm not a pussy," she said. *"But you'll delete them, right?"*

"Of course," I replied. *"What kind of guy do you think I am?"*

Obviously I didn't delete them. Deleting naked pictures a girl sends you is like being given a pan of baked ziti and throwing away the leftovers. I'm Italian and my family would consider that sacrilege.

Although she didn't ask, I reciprocated by sending her a picture of my cock. I photograph well and I like to show off the work.

"Wow. You like to hurt your victims, don't you?" she said.

"I just like to leave my mark," I responded.

"I can't wait for you to leave it on me."

"You look great naked."

"Thanks."

"How tall are you?"

"5'4…Petite. Yourself?"

"5'9."

"Very nice. Perfect size for me to get on my knees while you pull my hair and I gag on your cock."

"I couldn't agree more."

She asked me to come over, but I was in bed and in need of a manscape, so I declined and told her we'd get together soon. I fell asleep wondering if once the alcohol wore off, would she have inhibitions, or would it make her yearn for me more.

I got my answer the next morning when I woke up to find a Facebook message from her.

"Ha ha ha hope you wake up with a huge hard on!! ;)"

I was thinking about that message on the drive home from the evening's show in South Jersey, and as I started to get wood I sent her a text.

"Hey what's up?" I wrote.

"Fuck me," she replied.

Ah, what a nice girl. I'd manscaped earlier so I was ready to make a good impression. I headed to the Brooklyn dive bar that she'd been slopping around for the better part of the evening.

I had barely got out of the car before she jumped up on me, pushing me back against it and passionately mauling me like the love of her life had just returned from war. She grinded her pussy against my cock, reaching down and feeling my hard-on as if she wanted to make sure I hadn't lost it in battle. I kissed her, looking into her wide eyes, which looked beautiful even if they were a little bloodshot. She was sloppy drunk, but still looked cute and innocent.

I kissed her and spun us around so that she was up against the car. Pulling her tits out of her teal blouse, I felt the lovely handfuls and sucked on them. They had the perkiness and firm nature of fake tits but were clearly real. I sucked on her nipple, enjoying that first taste of tit, but then, out of the corner of my eye, I noticed some shady characters walking by.

Noelle lay back on the front of my Benz, sporting a sinister yet cute grin.

"Fuck me right here," she said, as she ground her nails into my sides.

"Ahh, ahh ... I would, but we might get shot. Let's get you outta the 'hood."

She smiled and kissed me, feeling the back of my hair and putting her tongue in my ear.

I drove us the few blocks to her apartment as Noelle kissed my neck, rubbing my cock the entire time.

Noelle led me up into her abode, grabbing my ass while sticking her hands inside my tight jeans and boxer briefs.

"You want me lick your ass?" she asked.

"No ... But we'll find something for you to do," I said.

Noelle responded by ripping my pants off and swallowing my cock like a fat guy trying to be inconspicuous as he devours a tray of free samples at the grocery store.

She had medium cock-sucking lips and they felt amazing as she undulated intensely, savoring all of my illustrious eight while cradling my balls and sucking on them as if they were cherry Jolly

Ranchers. I pulled her hair and pushed her head down.

"Oh Daddy, your cock tastes so good," she looked up and told me. "I'm choking on it."

She garbled some gibberish as she sucked me deeper and I jammed it down her throat. "That's so sweet of you," I said. "You fucking whore."

Some girls don't like being called degrading names, but given the fact that she was calling me "Daddy" and doing her best to "choke on my cock," I knew she was different.

Noelle was amazing—from the feel of her mouth to her rhythmically varying positions, intense passion and impeccable attention to detail. When I finally came in her mouth she gave a thorough pornstar swallow, guzzling the massive load with enthusiasm. It was one of the most awe-inspiring blowjobs I'd ever received. "Oh my God that was great," I said. "I'll be ready to go again in a few minutes."

We lay together on her bed, bullshitting, joking and flirting as anyone would on a first date.

"I usually get hard again quicker than this," I said as we shared a cigarette. "I had a long day— did a show and drove five hours—but I'll be ready to go again soon."

"You wanna wait till another day?" she asked.

"No, no," I said. "I just need a few minutes."

She let out a sigh as she lay back and smiled, looking at me like it was prom night and I was about to take her virginity. "I really like you James," she said. "You're cool."

"You're cool, too, baby," I said.

It was a genuine moment. Not the type of moment when you're coming on a girl's face, but something that could occur even if our genitals weren't on display. Noelle kept grabbing at my flaccid dong, but I still wasn't ready to go. I'm a guy who could go again and again, but she had sucked a lot out of me.

I fingered her. She felt so good—warm, gooey and sweet. I stuck my fingers in her mouth letting her slurp up her own secretions. Jealous of her enjoyment of the tasty treat I thought it was time I sampled it. I stuck my fingers back in her pussy and licked them. The sight of my enjoyment of her juice had already brought her near climax.

"Ohhh fuck me, Daddy!'" Noelle moaned as her eyes crossed.

Instead I continued to tease her pussy, waiting for my cock to get back into battle position.

"I want it so bad! Ohh ... Ohh," Noelle persisted.

As she lay back and pushed my head down with her hands, I stuck my face between her legs. I liked the way she pulled my hair while I licked her clit. In hindsight it probably wasn't the best idea to go down on a girl who had fucked me within minutes of meeting me, but damn, she had the best tasting cunt I ever ate. With some girls it was work to eat pussy—like eating a shitty meal at a relative's house—but this was something I'd pay for again and again even if it was overpriced.

"Oh god, James ... Oh ... Fuck me Daddy, fuck me!" Noelle grabbed her tit and sucked her finger.

I subtly rubbed my cock on the bed, desperately trying to harden as I ate her warm cunt and squeezed her ass. I slapped her buttocks as I shot my tongue up inside her.

"I'm almost there," I said, closing my eyes to conjure perverted thoughts and pressing my dong into the mattress.

I figured I could get her to where she was about to explode and then muster up some semblance of a hard-on inside her, and ride it out until she got off.

"I want that cock ... Give me that big dick, baby. Give me that big dick," Noelle insisted in her best phone sex operator voice.

I felt around, grabbing for my condom as my face remained buried in her crotch. I pulled up and got it open. Grabbing my cock for a few rubs, I pulled on the condom. My hard-on was back.

I pushed it inside her and began to thrust. The hardness immediately increased, taking me back toward maximum capacity. "Oh yeah, fucking so big, Daddy!" she yelled. Fucking so big."

I sucked her tits as I thrust. "Fuck me, Daddy! Fuck me!" she continued.

I was back at full gyration, squeezing her ass as I pushed my cock in and out of her stellar vagina.

"You like that, you whore?" I said. "Are you my fucking whore?"

"Yeah, Daddy, yeah," she panted. "Fuck. Fuck!"

"Come on whore, come on you fucking whore!"

I pulled her hair and thrust harder.

"Oh god," I said. "Your tight pussy feels so good you whore. You like it? You like my cock? Is it big, baby? Is it big?"

"It's so fucking big, Daddy! Fuck me with your big cock, Daddy!"

"That's right, you fucking whore! You're my fucking little slut! Little goddamn trollop ... You need to be punished, you bad little girl!"

"Punish me Daddy, punish me! I deserve it! I deserve it, Daddy!

I reared back, almost all the way out and then pushed back in, powerfully slamming her tight cunt repeatedly.

"Oh god," she said. "Hurt me Daddy! Hurt me! Ohhh...Ohhh."

"You like that," I said. "You fucking whore! You like that!"

I slapped her ass hard.

"Oh Daddy, I'm so fucking bad!" she said. "I'm so fucking bad. Am I your whore ... Am I your whore?"

She let out a squeal. If it had been any higher, only dogs could have heard it. "Oh yeah, you fucking whore!" I said.

I squeezed her ass tight as she dug her nails into my back, and continued her high-pitched moan. "Yeah yeah, yeah, yeah Daddy!"

She was coming so hard that she sounded on the verge of tears. I continued to thrust through it.

"Ohhh," Noelle moaned. "Ohhh ... Ohhh ... Ohhh."

"You coming, whore?" I said. "You coming for your Daddy?"

"I'm coming Daddy, I'm coming, I'm coming again."

I kissed her intensely, nibbling her lower lip as I thrust. The squeals continued until her constricting pussy ultimately pushed my cock out, leaving me soft and tired. I didn't get off, but she had three intense orgasms.

We lay next to each other, relishing the experience.

"Thank you, Daddy."

"You're Daddy's little whore, aren't you?

"Yes I am," she sighed. "Ohhh you're the best Daddy in the whole world."

"And don't you forget it."

Being a Lawyer Has its Perks

If being someone you're not will get you laid, I think it's your duty to do so. I'm not saying go through life like that, but the key is to fuck her and let the real you come out only when it's time to get rid of her

As I ordered a Vodka Cranberry at a swanky lounge in Tribeca a sultry redhead around my age began to look my way. The hair was coppery auburn, and the look was sexy and professional, like she was playing the domineering business woman in a cliché porno.

"Hi, how are you doing?" the Classy Broad asked.

"Doing well," I said. "Yourself?"

"Just having a few drinks," she said. "What have you been up to?"

"Just busy working."

"I know. I've been in court all week."

I surmised that she was a lawyer.

"How's your father," she asked.

"He's good," I said.

"Make sure you tell him I said hi."

"Of course. He'll like that."

She was flirty and touchy, her green eyes glistening as she looked at me. The vibe was there, but who the fuck was this broad? And how did she know my father?

"You remember the night we met at The Bubble Lounge?" she asked.

"Of course," I said.

"You were such an asshole to me."

Normally, I would think there was a very good chance that this statement was accurate, however I had no idea who the fuck she was. I'd also never been to the *The Bubble Lounge,* and knew for sure that even if my Dad was in the city, he'd never walk into a place called *The Bubble Lounge.* Regardless, she was hot, so...

"I was? I apologize. I'm so sorry. What happened exactly?"

"Well I was a making a big deal about your Dad because he's such an esteemed member of the legal profession, and you were just being obnoxious."

Although my father was a Renaissance man I was fairly confident that he hadn't gone to law school.

"Oh, well... I remember now," I said. "I was very drunk that night. That was my first night out in a while, my tolerance was low, and I had some shots. Please forgive me."

"We'll see about that," she said.

God, I hope I wasn't gonna have to make a grand gesture—like buy her a drink. The place was overpriced and it wasn't even like I had really been an asshole to her.

"What type of law do you focus on?" she asked me.

So not only was my father a lawyer, I was too. Well damn I came from a good family. I couldn't wait to tell my mother.

"Criminal litigation," I said.

"Me too."

"Well how 'bout that."

It was nice we had something in common, and I had seen every episode of *Ally McBeal* and *Boston Legal* so I was quite certain I could pull this off.

"I can't believe how cool you're being tonight," she said. "What a difference."

"Yeah... About that... I've always lived in my father's shadow. I've always been trying to keep up—and we were out that night to celebrate a case I just won, and as usual, the attention went to him, and I guess I took it personally and didn't react like I should have. For that, I'm sorry."

"It's okay, babe. I understand. But you're young. You keep working and you'll get to where your father is."

"I just wish he saw it that way."

She smiled, and I went in to kiss her. Her lips were soft and she knew exactly how to use her tongue—just enough, without being sloppy.

"You're a good kisser," she said.

"I doubt I'm as good as my Dad."

She laughed.

"I have to go hang out with my friends over there," she said, motioning her head to the left side of the bar.

"Okay," I said.

"You wanna come with me?"

"Sure."

We walked across the bar to join a few of her girlfriends. "Girls, this is Billy... Judge Maxwell's son."

"Hey. Hi. Nice to meet you, I'm Billy," I said. "Excuse me, I'll be right back."

Overcome with nerves I bolted for the bathroom to assess the situation. Okay, I was impersonating someone to get in with a girl but this wasn't like the time I pretended to be Stifler from *American Pie*, this was a judge's son. How much time could I get for this? All I kept thinking about was *Oz*, and the Aryan Brotherhood coming to ass rape me in my sleep. Okay, it was time to play it safe.

I walked out of the bathroom and back over to the lawyer broad and her friends.

"You wanna get outta here?" I whispered in her ear.

She smiled, finishing her martini in one gulp, and put her glass on the bar. "We're hungry, we're gonna get something to eat," she told the girls.

We walked downstairs, out of the lounge and up the sidewalk. "Where are we going? Your office?" she asked.

"We're remodeling my office right now, there's shit everywhere, but... You'll see."

"So where'd you go to law school?" she asked.

"University of Chicago," I said.

"Oh, I have a couple colleagues from there. Do you know Dante DeAndrea?"

"Don't think so."

"What about Greg Connelly?"

"I know the name. I kept to myself back then."

"Really? You?"

"I was in a very serious relationship with the law."

"I know how you feel."

"Let's not talk shop tonight. Let's have an adventure."

"I could use an adventure."

We walked a couple blocks to our destination. "Ooh, The Greenwich... Fancy," she said.

"That's right," I replied as I led her past the valet, and into the hotel lobby.

"Follow me."

We arrived at the location of our first-class accommodations, and I opened the door for my lady. I didn't want her knowing where I lived, since I was passing myself off as a judge's son and all

"Here we are," I said.

"This is the bathroom," she said, a dumbfounded look on her face.

"I know... The best in town."

"So you want to fuck me in the bathroom?"

"Uh huh," I said.

"That's so dirty."

"Is that a problem?"

"No."

I proceeded to maul her, my hands inside her gray tailored jacket as we kissed passionately, making our way into the bathroom. I picked her up by her ass and pushed through the door of the handicapped stall, slamming her against the wall and tore her white blouse opened, breaking the buttons, and exposing a perfect set of B-cups masked by a white bra. I squeezed those perfect handfuls, her thighs tensing up around me as she grinded her crotch into my hard cock.

I opened her bra from its front clasp, and sucked on her tits as I squeezed her ass and slammed her into the wall. She yanked the back of my head, pulling my hair hard as I took down her zebra print thong and undid my black slacks, pushing my pants and boxer briefs off. She grinded into me and I rubbed my hard cock against her clit, teasing her pussy as I prepared to enter her dripping muff.

"I don't do that," she said.

"What do you mean?" I asked.

"Stick it in my ass!" she demanded.

I quickly turned her around, and she immediately bent over pulling her skirt up, and laying her hands on the toilet seat. I slowly worked my index finger into her asshole, warming it up before adding a second finger. I grabbed my cock and eased into her ass, pushing gently little by little with a minor thrust.

"Oh god that hurts so good," she cried out.

I pushed in more, then slowly went further for a few strokes.

"Oh, oh, oh... Oh God yeah, I'm such a bad girl, I'm such a fucking ass whore," she insisted.

"I completely agree," I said.

I increased my pace pulling her hair as I vigorously drove my cock up her tight ass. "Fuck me, fuck my ass, pound it! Pound it hard!" she exclaimed.

I slid all the way in and stopped. She screamed and moaned so I did it again, and again, before smoothly going back to quickly pummeling her ass and forcefully spanking her. She rested on the toilet seat, pressing her face against it. It was dirty, raw, in-your-face, rock n' roll style fucking like it was meant to be done.

"You know how you were an asshole to me?" she said.

"Yeah."

"That's why I wanted to fuck you... Oh, oh!"

"I'm glad I was such a dick."

"I'm glad you got such a dick," she said. "Oh. Your big cock's gonna make me come, your big cock's gonna make me come.... Oh BILLY! BILLY! Make me your bitch, BILLY! Make me your little fucking whore!"

"Billy could do that," I said.

I put my arms around her waist pulling her back onto me as I kept driving my cock and pushed her down toward the toilet seat. "Yeah, yeah, fuck, fuck," she said with heavy breath, the ends of her hair lying in the bowl.

"You might wanna watch your hair there," I said.

"FUCK ME! FUCK ME! FUCK ME HARD!"

I reached around and inside her blouse squeezing her perky B cups, and rubbing her soaked clit as I pushed my dick all the way into her ass. She showed what an anal whore she was, taking all eight inches like a champ as I shoved two fingers into her slippery cunt.

"Take it... Take it all... You're such an ass whore. You're such a fucking ass whore."

"I am an ass whore," she said. "Oh God, fuck my ass! Oh god, I'm coming... I'm coming so fucking hard. Pound my ass. HARD! HARDER! OHH YEAH!"

I continued ramming her ass with long, fast, powerful thrusts as she climaxed. Her ass was so fucking tight I felt like I was going to pass out.

"I'm gonna come," I said. "I'm gonna come."

"You save that cum," she said. "You save it so I could taste it."

I pulled my hard dick out of her ass as her orgasm culminated. She turned around with moans of ecstasy, dropped to her knees and before I knew it, had shoved my hard cock into her mouth, swallowing it whole. She sucked hard, and

I grabbed the back of her head and pulled on her hair as I fucked her face.

"I'm fucking your face like the whore that you are," I said. "You fucking ass whore. You want my fucking cum? You want my cum? Oh... Oh yeah... Fuck... Oh."

My eyes crossed and I gasped for air as I shot my load in her mouth, my cock tingling as she sucked it all down. "Fuck oh yeah," I said. "God. Oh yeah. Ohh."

"Oh, oh yeah," she said. "I like that hot load all over my mouth."

"Well thank you. I worked hard on it."

"My ass tastes so good on your cock."

"I'll...take your word for it," I said, as she ran her tongue along my dong.

If I run into her again I'm telling her I made partner.

Latina Bad Girl

She was tied up on the ground on all fours, her hands and legs fastened around the legs of the sofa and love seat as I rubbed my hard cock against her face, and then moved to press it to her pussy and voluptuous ass.

Carmen and I had met at a bar and bonded over shared affection for dirty fucking without commitment. She'd sent over a drink, and then we piled into a cab. She straddled my cock while the car moved through the busy downtown streets toward my apartment, putting on a show for the turban wearing driver. Since we'd already come by the time we arrived at my building, she decided to call it a night.

I figured that would be all, and that was fine with me. But the next morning I woke up to a text where she was kind enough to thank me for my cock. In return, I told her I was much obliged for her fantastic pussy and the way it rode me like Lance Armstrong attacking the Pyrenees Mountains.

The dirty sexting continued all day culminating in a confession that she'd been a very bad girl and felt the only way to make up for her unsatisfactory behavior was for me to tie her up and spank her. Of course I agreed, because it was for her own good.

She came over to my place in Battery Park and stripped down to black fishnets, a thong, and heels.

"You better fucking leave marks," she said.

"I have to," I said. "How will you ever learn without discipline?"

Her dark bangs covered her eyes and round Latina ass was in the air as I tied white rope around her wrists and ankles tight enough that her circulation was cut off, leaving her in constant pain.

"This is gonna hurt you a lot more than it's gonna hurt me," I said as I stood in front of her with a sinister grin.

"It fucking better," she said. "If I start crying you better not stop."

"Do you want a safe word?" I said.

"No."

I paced back and forth around her, and gave her long hair a couple forceful yanks, rocketing her head back. I stood behind her admiring how good her high stilettos looked. I spat on her ass and reared my hand back to put a hard strike on her right cheek. I hit the left cheek, then the right again, and kept alternating. She begged for me to go harder, and I did. Then I started yanking her hair back and spanking her ass at the same time, her moans becoming louder and louder as her buttocks quivered.

"Oh, oh, oh, oh," she said. "I'm such a bad girl."

"Obviously."

I walked back in front of her and caressed her gently, softly rubbing her full red lips and chin. Then I choked her and grinded my hard cock against her face. I shoved the bottom of my balls in her mouth, feeling her tongue on them as she whimpered.

I walked around to the rear of her, taking a long look at her ass, and then stuck a finger in her cunt as I rubbed my cock between her spit-ridden ass cheeks. I slipped in another finger, and another and listened to her beg for me to satisfy her. She was so fucking wet when I finally put my cock inside her. That was just a tease, though. I pulled it out and slapped her ass with it hard, and listened to her plead with me some more before I went back inside.

I thrust in and out of her cunt with my hand squeezing the back of her neck choking her from behind, my balls ricocheting against her ass as I was about to come. I pulled out and moved in front of her. My hands were on the back of her head as I stood before her, fucking her face, my cock pressing against the back of her throat. I used my right hand to choke her as I admired the sounds of her gasping for air.

I jerked my cock, pushing it against her face, then stood in front of her stroking as she pleaded with me. "Not in the face," she begged. "Not in the face."

I blew copious amounts of cum all over her lips, cheeks, nose, eyes, even the long bangs that hung over her forehead. She licked around her mouth like a coke addict trying to taste the last remnants of powder.

"Untie me, James," she said. "Untie me so I could taste you."

I didn't answer her request, just sat on the couch in front of her with a nefarious look, watching as she craned her neck, and strained her tongue trying to lick up every drop of semen I splashed on her face.

Things were going well with Carmen but every time I talked to her it seemed like she'd been a bad girl, and I couldn't let her off without discipline. In other words, I liked our arrangement.

We kissed and I pressed her back against my counter, then turned her around and bent her over the kitchen table, pulling up the back of her red dress as she bent over with a red thong and garters. I pulled off my black belt and proceeded to whip her ass with it repeatedly, the leather clacking loud against her ass.

"Oh James, oh James," she said. "Harder, harder."

I struck her again, and again, then pressed my hard cock against her ass. I whipped her again, then ripped down her thong leaving her garters gripping her thighs as I thrust my cock into her warm pussy from behind. I took the belt to her ass as I fucked her hard, then put it around her neck, pulling her back and tightening it. She was gagging with my belt around her neck, clamoring for oxygen, and it was only making her pussy tighten.

She had four hard orgasms as I kept pounding her, blowing my first load inside her warm pussy then turning her onto the table, climbing on top, and choking her with my belt as I fucked her face. She gagged on my cock while her head pressed hard against the table, and she took down an abundant amount of cum.

Apparently the disciplining was never enough though because she required chastisement nearly every day for the next six weeks.

The Last Threesome

"I can't look at you without picturing your dick in her mouth," were the first words I heard that morning before I even opened my eyes, as I lay in bed hung over with a pee hard-on.

"Huh?" I yawned trying to unseal my eyes as the sun from the sky light burned a hole in my retina and noticed Carmen looking down at me with an even stronger vengeance. "What the fuck happened?"

"You heard me," she said. "I can't look at your without picturing your dick in her mouth."

"You said watching a girl suck my dick was a fantasy of yours," I said in utter dismay, still trying to wake up.

"Yeah, a fantasy," she said. "But to actually see it ... was torture."

"Oh," I groaned as I sat up, and reached for a smoke. "You seemed to be into it last night."

I took the day's first drag.

"Well ... yeah," she said. "But now I think about it ... and I'm grossed out."

"I think you're thinking too much."

"Did you enjoy it?" she asked.

"Of course I enjoyed it ... Why wouldn't I enjoy it? It's a blowjob."

"You liked it?"

"Um ... Well you know," I pulled myself out of bed and stood up, my cock still rock hard. "It was okay... You're the one, though."

I grasped her hands and passionately gazed into her eyes, continuing with my performance. "When my cock's ... in *your* mouth, it means something."

"Awww... You're so sweet."

I put my arms around her and we hugged. I pushed my cock against her pelvis.

"Stop!" she said, pushing me away.

I didn't see what the big deal was. We had a threesome. And the girl was really hot. It wasn't like I asked her to have a fat chick sit on her face— I could see how that would've been torture—but Carmen had even picked the girl.

What made this threesome different was that I'd kind of let Carmen believe that she was my girlfriend.

She had long told me—for the six weeks I knew her (it was a long-term fake relationship)— that it was one of her fantasies for me to make her watch as "some whore"—her words, not mine...I have a little more respect—sucked my cock. I try to be as giving a fake boyfriend as I can, so I did everything in my power to make that dream come true. You'd think she'd be happy, but no.

We had settled in at a downtown restaurant the night before. A long-legged busty blond server who looked like she just stepped out of the pages of a Victoria's Secret catalogue took our drink order.

"You think she's hot, don't you?" Carmen asked as our server walked away.

"No ... of course not ... You know I don't look at other women in such a lewd way."

"Well, I think she's hot."

"You know, on second thought I agree with you."

"Second thought?"

"Well, actually, I thought you were talking about a different girl."

"Which one?"

"I don't know."

"Watch this, Wingman."

Carmen began walking toward our waitress, who stood at the bar waiting for drinks. I wondered if I should follow or stay put. Always smooth and assertive, Carmen appeared to have a plan, and I certainly didn't want to cockblock my own cock. He would never forgive me.

While Carmen and the girl talked, the two of them were looking over at me. I did my best to appear ruggedly sexy as I sipped my sugar-free Red Bull and vodka. Derek Zoolander had nothing on me. I wanted to act like I didn't notice, but I needed to gauge the reaction. Our server had a sly smile on her face. No drool dripped from her lip, but I could tell she was holding it back in order to keep up appearances.

She and Carmen were already getting touchy-feely, caressing each other's arms as they flirted. I could have jerked off alone at the table, but much like the bimbo—I mean, *waitress*—I wanted to keep up appearances, as well as avoid arrest. Carmen returned to the table with a cocky smile on her face reminiscent of the one I wear when I grab a girl's digits.

"Looks like I'm The Wingman tonight," she said.

"We all need a night off. So what's the deal?"

"Use your imagination."

"Okay...Well, maybe I should wait because otherwise I won't be able to walk out of here."

"That's true ... But I like it when you're hard in public."

"That's why I'm here with you. And a little hard."

Carmen slowly reached under the table, rested her hand on my leg, and grazed my crotch. "That's more than a little, babe," she said.

"Well, thank you," I said.

We were going to rendezvous at Carmen's, directly across the street, after our new friend got off work. We had bottles of Champagne and Grey Goose on ice, ready to go.

I went into the bathroom to jump up and down. Not because I was excited—I needed to stretch and get the creative juices flowing.

The buzzer went off and Carmen came up. When Crystal, our party guest arrived at the door, she was still in her work clothes: a sexy black blouse that showed off her fantastic rack, tight black booty shorts, and stiletto boots.

"Hey girl," Carmen said as she hugged her hello.

"Hi," Crystal replied.

"Hey," I said.

"Would you like a drink?" Carmen asked.

"Love one," Crystal said.

We sat down and relaxed and talked over vodka tonics.

Carmen began mauling the blond, who towered over her, and violently slammed her against the wall. "Ahhh!" Crystal screamed.

As Crystal kissed Carmen they pulled hair, wrestling to strip each other down. Then Carmen took charge and ripped Crystal's clothes off. She climbed her, doing pull-ups on her massive tatas like she was in the middle of an intense workout and I was her personal trainer.

"Another one ... You've got it in you ... but pace yourself," I would've advised.

Carmen and Crystal kissed passionately, and Carmen sucked on Crystal's perfect *Playboy* nipples, while firmly squeezing her tits.

I came up behind Carmen, kissing her neck and fingering her wet pussy from the back as she worked on Crystal. Putting my left hand between the girls, I slowly rubbed Crystal's clit as I fingered Carmen with the right.

"Oh god," Crystal said. "Oh that feels good."

I stuck my fingers in Crystal's warm pussy. She was sopping wet and only getting wetter. These girls could have kept a village in a desert irrigated with their secretions.

"I want you to suck my man's cock," Carmen said.

"I wouldn't argue with her," I said. "She's a feisty little one."

"Oh yeah," Crystal said. "I want to suck your fucking cock. Show it to me."

I dropped my pants and stood in my black boxer briefs. My cock was ready to burst through like a fat girl's ass straining to escape from a scandalous Halloween costume. Crystal rubbed and sucked my shaft through the fabric, covering my boxer briefs in saliva.

"Oh god," I moaned.

"You got a great cock," Crystal said.

"Thanks," Carmen and I said simultaneously.

Crystal used her teeth to pull off my underwear and start licking my cock. Carmen was nice enough to help.

I rose to my feet as the two beauties remained on their knees sucking and rubbing. They locked lips as they took turns putting my cock in their mouths like it was a joint they were passing back and forth.

Carmen started to back away.

"Suck his cock!" she demanded. "Suck that cock, bitch!

"Okay," Crystal agreed.

"Make my man come!" Carmen continued.

"Oh yeah," Crystal said.

"Jesus," I said. "Won't, won't be long."

Carmen sat on the bed and played with her pussy, sliding her fingers in and out and swirling her clit with her index and middle fingers.

Meanwhile she looked on as Crystal gagged on my hard-eight.

"Yeah, Crystal, suck his cock, suck his big fucking cock, yeah," Carmen exclaimed. "Oh. You like that, James? You like the way the bitch sucks your cock? Oh ... oh ... oh..."

Carmen continued moaning and screaming out.

"Oh yeah, baby," I said. "Oh yeah."

"Oh ... oh ... oh, gag on it, bitch!" Carmen screamed "Are you gagging on it?"

Crystal came up, licking the shaft, using her tongue to dab the tip of my heaving dong. "I'm gagging on your man's big cock," she said. "Oh yeah."

And she put it back in her mouth, where it belonged, racing up and down. I savored her wet full lips as she gagged some more on my cock.

"Give her that tasty load," Carmen said. "Give it to her."

"Oh god ... Oh ... That's ... good," I said. "Fuck, yeah!"

"Aaah," Crystal said.

"Faster, faster, fucking faster," I said.

"Yeah, that's right bitch," Carmen said. "Suck his big cock."

"I'm coming," I exclaimed. "I'm coming, I'm coming!"

My hot load rocketed out of my cock. I felt like it was going to shoot Crystal across the room but she kept sucking, and swallowing, savoring every drop.

"I'm coming, I'm coming, I'm coming!" Carmen cried out as she jammed her fingers into her slippery snatch.

"That's so hot, baby," I said.

"Tastes so good," Crystal said.

"Oh," I said. "Oh yeah."

"Aaaahhhhhh," Carmen said. "Oh yeah ... Yeah."

"Eat my girl's cunt, eat my girl's pussy," I demanded as I pulled Crystal's hair.

"Yeah, yeah, I will," she said.

Crystal got on the bed, buried her head between Carmen's legs, and began to lick her wet pussy. She fired her tongue up inside her as I looked in on in awe and amusement.

"That's right ... That's right," I said. "Just give me a minute, girls."

I gasped for air, and smiled as I reveled in what I was experiencing as the headliners took the stage.

"Crystal, eat my girl's pussy," I said. "Eat it up."

"I want it bad," Crystal said. "I wanna eat your pussy."

"How's my cunt taste?" I said, obviously in reference to the vagina that was currently under my jurisdiction, even if it was a fake one.

"So good," Crystal moaned without taking a breath.

"Oh, oh," Carmen said.

"Eat that pussy," I said. "Eat that cunt. This is one fucking great show."

The two girls continued going at it, and within a couple of minutes I had recovered.

"I'm ready to go again," I said.

"I don't know," Carmen said. "Should we give him another go?"

"Hmm," Crystal pondered. "Well, he's your man."

"Well you're company," Carmen said. "Do you want him?"

"Naw," Crystal said.

"What?" I said.

"I'm fucking with you," Crystal said.

I looked into Carmen's eyes as I pushed her knees behind her head.

"You're so sexy, baby," I said.

"So are you, baby," she said.

I railed Carmen as Crystal was sucking on her tits, and kissing the both of us. I came but didn't acknowledge it and kept going.

"Keep going baby, keep going," Crystal said. "How does he do that?"

"Practice makes perfect," I said.

"Oh yeah," Carmen said. "He learned by fucking lots of whores."

"Wow," Crystal said. "There must have been a lot of whores."

"Am I better?" Carmen said. "Am I better than those whores? Do I fuck better than those whores?"

"Well, duh," I said.

As they both lay on the bed I alternated eating one pussy and fingering the other, back and forth.

"Stick it in me," Crystal said. "Stick it in."

"Give it to her," Carmen said.

"I just came three times," I said. "Give me a minute."

"Help him," Crystal said. "Help him ... Ohhhhh."

Carmen's smooth lips wrapped around my cock, and I was immediately back to full mast.

"Suck it," I said. "Suck it."

"Don't be rude," Carmen said. "We have a guest."

"I will accommodate her momentarily," I said.

"Fuck me," Crystal said. "Fuck me! Fuck me!"

Crystal lay on the floor on her back, as I prepared to mount her and Carmen stepped over her, straddling her in front of me so I could study her ass while I thrust into Crystal. Carmen and Crystal kissed, wedging their tits inside each other's as they reached down and worked each other's clits while I held Carmen's hips and heaved my rock-hard dong into Crystal's soaked pussy. I pulled out of Crystal and pushed my cock into Carmen, fucking her doggy style as Crystal sucked her tits. I pulled my dick out and went back into Crystal while Carmen's ass bounced in front of me and she nibbled Crystal's hard nipples. I alternated cunts twice more and was ready to fucking bust.

The walls of Crystal's pussy were closing as she reached orgasm again. I tried to keep my cock in but her tight cunt pushed it right out.

"Oh god," Crystal said. "You're so fucking good. So good, James."

"Oh god," I said. "I'm gonna come! I'm gonna come! Who wants it?"

I pulled my dick out and blew my load all over Carmen's ass. "Here try it," Carmen said, and sat on Crystal's face allowing her lips to taste my warm sperm on her ass.

"You like my man's cum?" Carmen asked.

"So good ... So fucking good!" Crystal said as she breathed heavy, her heart pounding. She savored the flavor like a snob sampling wine in an exclusive bistro.

After a night so beautiful, the next morning was hell.

"James, I can't see you anymore," Carmen said.

"That's fucking ridiculous," I said. "Did you notice I got you off before I got her off? That should go for something."

"I know, you're sweet ... but ... I can't do this."

"We don't have to do it again."

"I don't mean that. I'm just not, ready for a relationship."

"Well, neither am I," I said telling her the absolute truth for once. "But was I bad in the threesome?"

"James."

"No, really, was I bad? Was something off? We'd been drinking. And two girls is a lot to handle … even for me."

"You were great."

"Then what's the problem?"

"I can't look at you the same way."

"I did it for you."

"I know. You were so sweet. But we're over, James."

"Do we fuck again, first?" I said.

Carmen hugged me and gave me a kiss on the cheek, then took a long look at me as she began to tear up.

"Is that a yes?" I asked.

And that's how I was dumped by my pretend girlfriend. I walked out of her building's lobby, threw my tan jacket over my shoulder, and lit a cigarette as I strolled along Wall Street, slowing taking a drag—reminiscing and wondering what had just happened. I vowed then I'd never have a threesome again.

I changed my mind two weeks later, but at the time, I vowed.

The Girl Next Whore 2

The bed shook as I railed Noelle doggy style, pulling her hair, squeezing her hips and slapping her ass like she was one of Bing Crosby's kids.

"Fuck me! I'm a bad girl! Fuck me harder! Fuck me harder, James!" she said as I pushed my cock in and out of her warm, wet pussy, grasping her hips so as not to send her into a head on-collision with the wall.

"Come on, you whore!" I said. "Fucking whore! Fuck yeah. You like that?"

"Hurt me baby! Fucking hurt me!"

"I'll fucking hurt you. Put you in pain."

"Give it to me! I want the pain! I want the pain! I wanna hurt!"

"I'm gonna make you so sore! I'm gonna make you so fuckin' sore!"

There was a pounding at the door. "Could you guys please quiet down?!" her roommate Sara barked from the other room.

"Sorry," I said.

"Don't be sorry ... FUCK ME!"

"What do you think I'm doing—cuddling with you and telling a story?"

"Pound my pussy! Pound my pussy!" she gasped for air. "Pound ... Pound ... Pound."

"You like that bitch? You like that? Are you my whore? Daddy's little whore."

"You're my daddy, you're my daddy!! And I'm your bad little girl."

"I can't believe you'd say that. That is so hot!"

"I'm your whore ... I'm your whore ... I'm your whore of a teenage daughter."

"That's awesome."

The mattress was springy and Noelle collided with the lamp, knocking it off the nightstand. She flipped around, and I lay her on her back on the nightstand. There was no time to move back to the bed, and I slid my hard cock back into her soaked cunt.

"Fuck me Daddy."

"Well, I was trying to."

I fucked her missionary style, on the tiny table surface. I held her to keep her from falling as I was inches from slipping off the mahogany.

There was another pound at the door. "Could you please quiet down?!" Sara said, obviously annoyed.

"We're being as quiet as we can," I yelled.

"She's so jealous," Noelle said quietly.

"Of what?" I asked.

"She wants to fuck you."

"Oh ... Well I'm sorry I was so mean to her."

"She broke up with her boyfriend and she really thinks you're hot. I showed her a picture of your cock."

I pulled Noelle's hair.

"Ahh ... Ahhh ... Ahh," she said.

"You showed her a picture of my cock? That's so nice of you ... What'd she think?"

"She really liked it."

"Tell her I said thanks. That was kind of her to say."

"Fuck me hard!"

"I'm so glad to hear that I brightened her day."

"I said fuck me!"

"Okay."

"Yeah ... Give it to me!"

Noelle sat on my cock, riding me reverse-cowgirl as I lay on the bed. We had a smooth pace going. She'd already gotten me off several times so I was into a solid groove. This horny broad would push me to new levels. Her ass looked so sexy while she rode me as I held her hips tight.

"So your roommate wants to fuck me?" I said.

"Uh huh."

"Well ... Why don't we invite her in?"

"What?"

"Come on ..."

"No."

"Hey your roommate's going through a very tough time right now."

"Right."

"So, do you not like her?"

"I love her. She's my BFF."

"Well if you love her, and she's feeling down, we really should invite her in."

"No ... I love her... That's why I don't want her anywhere near you."

"I guess you weren't raised to share."

"No it's not that, it's ... I ..."

"Look at it this way..."

Noelle continued riding me as I squeezed her ass and moved her back and forth.

It was like we were having a business meeting over an orgasm—well, several orgams. Noelle dismounted and lay down on her back, and I quickly re-inserted my cock and continued my work.

"I know you care about your roommate, and I know what it's like to go through a rough breakup, and if I ... if we ... Could take her away from that pain for a few minutes ... We owe it to her."

"Ugh."

"Of course I'll be thinking about you the whole time."

Noelle grabbed me by the back of my head and kissed me.

"She might want you to come on her face."

"If I have to I will."

I kissed Noelle. It was on, and I was psyched. A few minutes later, we walked out of the room to find Sara sitting on the couch, cuddled up in a blanket with her white Maltese puppy as she flipped channels. Her hair was long, dark and curly. Like Noelle, her tits were perfect Cs, but she had a darker, edgier way about her. At the moment she was mopey, her eyes bloodshot. I could see she was full of anger and boiling beneath the surface. She looked at us, puzzled.

"Sara," I said. "I just wanted to apologize for how rude I was."

"Just be considerate," she said. "You know, I live here, too."

"Of course. I would never want to disrespect your space in such a manner."

"It's okay."

"Would you mind if I sat down?"

"Go ahead."

Sara rolled her eyes as I sat down by her on the couch, and turned to her. "I want to make it up to you," I said.

"What are you gonna do?" Sara asked.

"Just hear him out," Noelle said.

"I just really don't feel like talking," Sara said.

While Noelle whispered to Sara I unbuttoned my jeans and started pulling them down.

"What are you doing?" Sara said. "What's he doing?"

I dropped my pants, exposing my cock.

"Being considerate," I said.

"What the fuck?" Sara said.

"He is, Sara," Noelle said. "He's being very considerate."

"Uh huh," Sara muttered as her eyes widened.

She was blushing. Surprisingly there was an awkward silence in the room as I sat there with my pants off, my flaccid dong flying free, and then Sara burst out laughing.

"What are you?" I said. "You're not laughing at the size, are you?"

"No," Sara said.

"I'm a grower, not a shower. Tell her Noelle."

"We love the size, Daddy," Noelle said. "Right, Sara? You saw his picture."

"It's very nice," Sara said.

"Okay. Good. And thank you."

We all shared a laugh

"Sara," I said, "don't be nervous."

"Don't be, baby," Noelle said.

"I'm not," Sara said.

"This is all about you," I said.

"What do you mean?" Sara said.

I looked deep into her brown eyes and whispered, "Suck my dick, bitch."

Sara was silent, taking this in, her face getting red while Noelle nodded in approval. Sara grabbed my cock, which was now on a break, and started to lightly rub it. She played with my dick and licked the sides, allowing me to gradually harden. She moved to the floor and got on her knees, beginning to swallow my cock.

"Ahh, ahh, take it easy," I said. "Pace yourself. Now that's good. Uh-huh."

I was getting my dick sucked by Sara, and Noelle sat next to me on the couch kissing me. I squeezed and sucked her tits as Sara's mouth went up and down on my cock.

"Oh god, James ... Oh," Noelle said.

Sara continued to go back and forth, savoring my cock as she gagged on it.

"See, isn't this making you feel better?" I said.

"Shut up and fuck me!" Sara said.

"Fine."

Sara bent over the recliner, her ass up in the air, slapping it. "Put your cock inside me," she demanded.

I love when a girl is demanding in the bedroom, or the living room for that matter. It shows passion.

Noelle hurried to the other side of the couch, kissed Sara and then sucked her tits as I proceeded to fuck Sara slowly. I'd already come several times and didn't know how much I had left.

"Faster, faster, faster," Sara said.

"I'm pacing myself. Chill."

Noelle and Sara passionately kissed as I continued to thrust and squeeze Sara's round breasts.

"Oh yeah, Sara," I said. "Oh yeah."

I kissed the side of Sara's neck as Noelle continued to suck her tits. Then Noelle and I locked eyes, and she rushed around the couch to my side.

"I need a word with you," she mouthed the words silently as I continued thrusting into Sara from behind.

"In a minute," I mouthed.

"Now," Noelle mouthed.

I continued thrusting in and out of Sara as the silent conversation carried on between Noelle and me.

"I can't stop," I mouthed.

"What are you doing yelling her name?" Noelle mouthed.

"Ugh ... I was fucking her."

"You said you only want me?"

"Well, I do."

"It doesn't seem that way."

"It's common etiquette ... You, say the name of the girl your dick's in. It's good manners."

Sara interrupted, screaming even louder. "Fuck me ... See asshole I'm getting fucked! I'm getting fucked! This is a real dick. This is what a real fucking cock feels like you fucking tic-tac...Tic-tac ... Dong."

"I'm not Tic-Tac dong," I said.

"Fuck me dammit!" Sara said. "Make me your bitch!"

Noelle and I looked at each other, smirking and laughing quietly, as the fucking advanced.

"Sara, would you sit on my face?" Noelle said.

Noelle lay down on her back on the couch.

"Oh yeah, oh yeah" Sara said as she came hard against my cock. "Oh! Yeah, yeah, yeah."

After Sara got off, she got off me quickly finding solace mounting Noelle's face like it was a trusty stead she was ready to ride through the Rocky Mountains.

Noelle slipped her head out from under her ass. "James," she said. "Put your cock inside me."

I fucked Noelle missionary style as Sara sat on her face, swaying. Sara moved to kiss me in the process but I pulled my head back, screaming extra loudly, "Oh Noelle, you're so hot, oh Noelle! Come on Noelle!"

"Oh Noelle," Sara said. "Oh Noelle ... Oh ... Eat my pussy. Eat my cunt. Oh, oh, you're so my BFF!"

"Mine too," I said.

I stood in front of Sara, stroking my cock fast.

"Blow it on her face," Noelle yelled. "Blow it on her face."

"I don't know if I have any left," I said.

Sara was on her knees with her mouth wide open as I rubbed my cock hard.

"Ugh," I said, "I guess I do. Oh yeah. Oh."

"Give it to me," Sara said. "Give it to me!"

"My cum will cleanse you of your despair."

I stroked my dick hard and fast and shot my warm and powerful load all over Sara's face. My cock stung like a motherfucker.

"Oh... Oh yeah," Sara said. "Feels so good. Yeah yeah."

"Oww," I said in pain. "Oww ... Yeah."

"That's right, girl," Noelle said. "That's right. You feel better?"

"Oh yeah," Sara slurred. "Taste it. It's so good."

"I'm not tasting it," I said.

"Not you, asshole," Noelle said.

Noelle slowly helped lick my cum off her BFF's face, and then they locked their cum-slicked lips together, kissing passionately, savoring the flavor, while a few drops dribbled to the floor.

My mother always said I was selfish. Well, Mom, not anymore. I felt good knowing that despite the great pain brought on by my many ejaculations I was still able to make poor Sara feel better. Mom, that money shot was for you.

Courting Crazy

You're probably wondering why my arrangement with Noelle didn't sour after our threesome with her BFF the way that my fake relationship with Carmen did. It's very simply really. Unlike Carmen, Noelle had never claimed to be bisexual. Forming an emotional attachment— even a fake attachment—to a woman who proclaims to be bisexual is like banging a girl who holds a stick of dynamite in her hand. While every guy dreams of a girl who craves box, once you've come, it's just another weapon she could use against you that the straight broads don't have. If she gets pissed at you, she'll just turn lesbian.

You don't pay enough attention to me, you were mean to my friends, you leave the toilet seat up ... Fuck you, I like girls now!

Like most girls Vicky was an undiagnosed schizophrenic possessing a variety of offbeat characters that could come out at any given time. Figuring out who I might get was like a game of high stakes Russian Roulette.

I'd say she had five to seven distinct personalities, and there were a couple of them I really didn't care for. But if you don't like one person in a group of friends, does that mean you can't be friends with any of them? This wasn't junior high.

It was same thing with Vicky except all the people were crammed into one tiny five-foot-two-inch body. There was the whore I like, the whore I don't like, the sweet and cute girl-next-door, the abstinent prude, the crazy bitch, and the Vietnam vet hell-bent on killing people. The only thing that sucked was I couldn't use a wingman to handle the bad apples of the group.

We could have a lot of fun when she was, say the sweet and cute girl next door, but then there was the cold-blooded cunt who would get angry and throw glass bottles at my head. When she was around, I'd mind my own business and tell her, "I have to get going. The person you were yesterday, have her call me."

And eventually a personality that I enjoyed would resurface and we'd engage in some good old fashioned hate-fucking. To be more specific, we'd engage in violent lubeless anal while I called her a cunt. It was anger management therapy for me, and judging by the way she'd scream she was reaping benefits as well.

We had just had a tremendous round of daytime sex, and were laying in my bed when one of her other personalities appeared.

"You're amazing," I told her.

You're getting too boyfriendy," she replied.

"You just went down on me... Would you prefer I said 'thanks whore, how much do I owe you?'"

"James, I've been thinking about this for a long time," she said. "I'm a … lesbian."

"But what about... What we just did?" I asked.

"What about it?"

"I just went down on you … You seemed to enjoy the accommodations."

"Lesbians go down on each other."

"Okay."

"I have never had an orgasm from sex."

"A lot of girls don't. You get them from the other stuff."

"Yeah … But so do lesbians."

"What about when you kiss me?"

"You know who kisses … Lesbians. I think about other girls when I'm hooking up with you."

"I think about other girls when I'm hooking up with you. I like big boobs."

"James … I don't even like giving head."

"You think you're the first girl I've met who doesn't like giving head. Are they all lesbians?"

She told me a lesbian friend of hers, Erin, had told her that she has emotional connections with guys but isn't into them sexually.

"Don't you find me attractive?" I asked.

"Yes I find you attractive," Vicky said. "But she said it's okay to find guys attractive."

"This is bullshit! You're not a lesbian! You're bi. You've always been bi. What does this fucking cockblocker know?"

"She's a lesbian. She knows, James. You don't."

Apparently if a lesbian tells another girl she's a lesbian, they are, that's it, end of story. It's gospel. They must turn a lot of hot chicks.

"Then what if I hook up with your friend Ashley?" I asked.

"I don't care James. I'm gay. I don't get what you don't understand."

"Well ... You liked me an hour ago."

She's wasn't a lesbian, she was a masochist. And that's in addition to being a cunt—a personality quality she was quite proud of.

Not long after that, Vicky had a "coming out party" and then began having a torrid love affair with Erin, the one who had made her realize that she was a lesbian. I knew that bitch was just trying to get into Vicky's pants. I wouldn't have cared except that Erin wasn't quite as into the concept of commitment free moments as I was. Personally, I felt the three of us should get together and work this out like adults, by having threesomes, provided her girlfriend and I took turns getting the check. It's only fair. Why should I pay for both of them?

"She doesn't do threesomes," Vicky told me. "That's slutty. And no, you can't watch. That's for fake bisexuals who only hook up with girls for attention. That's like you watching me with another guy."

I begged to differ, but what was I gonna say?

"Oh yeah, that's cool because I'm more into dudes now anyway... Yeah. But I don't do threesomes unless it's with all guys. And no, you can't watch. I'm not the kind of guy who just does other dudes for attention. I'm drawn to cock."

Yeah, that doesn't work. It's not as cool for straight guys to intermingle with each other. Girls have such an advantage.

Overcome with anger, my bisexual competition accosted me near the doorway of a bar on Bleeker. She was as hot and curvy as she was jealous. She had wide hips and shoulders, with breasts like boxing gloves. With a couple inches on me, and a couple more in heels, the possessive pussy hound towered over me.

"Stay away from her!" my Bisexual Competition demanded. "We have something going. She's happy."

"Relax," I said. "I'm cool with whatever you guys wanna do. In fact, I know you like guys, too. So if you'd be up for a threesome, I'd be willing to step up and be the man."

I had to see for myself.

"Oh you would?" she said.

"We both care about Vicky a great deal. Let's do this for her," I said. "It's what we all want."

"You like my boobs?"

"They're pretty awesome. Your parents must be very proud."

"Come here," she said, motioning to her tatas.

"Would it be weird if I called you Mom?"

She pressed her left D-cup—rather perky for a natural boob that size—into my mouth. My eyes closed as I enjoyed the taste of teat as if I were a malnourished Somalian baby clamoring for the last sip of milk.

The impassioned blonde bombshell fiercely jerked her knocker upward, slamming into my top front teeth, shooting a sharp pain to my septum. Instantly, she fired a combination of bruising cheap shots that bounced me off the wall like a prizefighter against the ropes, and used a final haymaker to send me to the ground. On my knees, I wiped my mouth, watching blood trickle to the floor as she stood over me.

"Stay away from my girl, you little bitch!" she proclaimed as rage emanated from her glistening blue eyes. "This relationship's not open. She belongs to me! Next time I'll kill you."

As I stumbled painfully onto the sidewalk, making sure my perfect teeth were still in place, I wondered if my commitment-free romance had reached its expiration date. And I realized I still wasn't finished fighting for that threesome.

Despite my Bisexual Competition's assault on me, Vicky and I continued to get together.

I definitely didn't trust her, and she admitted she didn't believe a word I said, but for a few hours every once in a while we would pretend. It's like buying a lap dance from a stripper you feel like you connect with, knowing full well that if you're not too careful she'll steal your wallet. Still, you enjoy the conversation she has with you as she blows in your ear while she vehemently gyrates against your crotch.

I eventually decided that it was time for a long overdue session with my sex therapist.

Sandy was a fan of mine who'd approached me a few years back after a show telling me she thought I could benefit from her treatments. A sex therapist, and admitted crazy bitch, she thought regular sessions with her could be beneficial to a man who deals with the array of unbalanced broads I tend to bed.

I was never one for therapy, but she looked more like a high-class escort than Dr. Ruth so I figured I'd give her a chance. She was offering her services pro-bono and it would have been rude to decline.

When I showed up for my first session I was skeptical and figured I'd more than likely pass the time by admiring the brunette cougar's voluptuous breasts but actually found her methods to be therapeutic in helping me me purge my soul, and get a better grasp on my feelings. So I decided to continue my sessions—especially in instances like this, where I was afraid that I'd altered a girl's sexual preference.

I sat on Sandy's couch full of stress, telling her my latest issue with Vicky.

"You need to relax, babe," Sandy said as she unzipped my Armani jeans.

"How the fuck could she be a lesbian?" I said. "Did I drive her that way? Is my dong not as great as I thought it was?"

Sandy slurped it up.

"Your dong is outstanding, James."

Sandy went back to blowing me.

"Well thanks," I said. "I know it is, but it's nice to hear."

"She's absolutely one hundred percent not a lesbian," Sandy said, then proceeded to lick my balls. "It's a combination of the shock value of getting the attention that she needs, and pushing away from her true emotions about the situation."

And, I was back in her mouth.

"Oh God," I yelled out, my mouth opened wide as my eyes crossed. "I really like therapy!"

I took a couple breaths, my semen pushing up to the head of my cock. "Over and over she insists she doesn't want a relationship, then she tries to push to get close only to turn back into a psycho bitch," I said, as I began to breathe even more heavily.

"Then, then, then … Oh god … Then… Then she calls all the time ..Oh yeah … Then she just fucking pulls away again," I said. "This is really helping. Oh God."

I panted, and Sandy lifted her head.

"She pulls away because she is trying to become unattached as far as her emotions are concerned," Sandy said. "She says that she doesn't want to be in a relationship, but she really does."

Sandy rode on top of me, my hands tightly grabbing her hips, her big tits bouncing up and down with every thrust.

"I have concluded that the reason why she can't form a healthy relationship is her insecurity, which has to do with a problem with her family," Sandy said. "She sabotages relationships because she doesn't think she's good enough."

"Meanwhile the timing was too convenient, since the "coming out party" took place just a few days before her six-week winter break came to an end and she had to head back to Queens Community for her final semester of college. Even though it was local, with classes and a job her stress level had her on the verge of a breakdown almost daily. For instance, even though she hated cigarettes—despised my smoking—on her first day back to school she suddenly started calling herself a "chain smoker," I added.

Sandy continued to ride me.

"Vicky's going back to school, so she knows she's going to have some kind of distance, whether it's physical or not," she said."

Sandy and I lay in each other's arms as I explained my issues with Vicky's friends.

"She doesn't even like this cunt, Sasha, but now they're hanging out all the time," I said. "The other night when Vicky was getting ready to sing at an open mic , I was trying to talk to her—this was the night of her new-found revelation—and Sasha wouldn't stop interrupting and insulting me."

"You wanna talk about the ultimate cockblock, that's Sasha. Instead of getting actual reassurance from a real friend, Vicky's getting the negative reassurance to act insane. Now it's time to return the favor."

And so, my sex therapist sat on my face.

I eased my head out from under her.

"So what do I do?

"Nothing," Sandy said.

"Nothing?"

"She's a crazy bitch and it's always going to be up and down, and honey, you deserve a lot better. So just cut her off—totally."

"So just do nothing?"

"Well, not just nothing," she said. "Eat my pussy."

And with those words I blocked Vicky's number and Facebook, and realized I'd reached the expiration date on commitment free moments with the crazy bitch. Thank God for therapy.

Texting Won't Stifle My Adventure

She didn't look up from her phone.

"Yeah that's cool," she laughed, then intensely typed into the touch screen of her iPhone.

I sat across the table from Aubrey in a swanky Asian fusion spot in the financial district as she ate her spicy tuna roll with her hands, dipping the pieces in soy sauce like she was eating mozzarella sticks and marinara sauce. "So I really like you," she said, her eyes still glued to her phone and fingers rapidly typing.

"You too," I mustered a smile.

She had a way of saying words that were supposed to mean something while avoiding eye contact completely, and continuing to multitask. Her mouth opened wide with surprise, and she used both hands to passionately type, smiling as she pressed "Send". "Would you prefer I text you so we could have a better conversation?" I asked.

"What?" she laughed, awkwardly. "Oh Jen had something really important to tell me, and then Abigail was totally freaking out about this older guy she's been off and on with, and Marissa was telling me that she fucked him, too. But, Abigail didn't know, so I was telling Abigail."

"That might mean more to me if I knew the people," I said.

Truthfully it wouldn't. I didn't care. Young girls did that all the time, though, where they'd mention their friends by first name as if the person they're telling knows their life story. They were wannabe socialites and in their opinions Facebook and Twitter celebrities who thought everybody wanted to know the intense reality show soap opera that was their awesome lives. I'd say this was a New York thing, or a city thing, but every small town had the same cliques of girls in their late teens and early twenties.

"So you're like, writing a book?" she asked.

"Uh huh."

"I hate reading."

"That honestly doesn't surprise me."

She ate another roll with her left hand while continuing to type with her right. That must be her dick hand, I thought. She extended her arm across the table shoving her iPhone in my face, scrolling through drunken pictures of her and her friends holding drinks, and dancing. "Look, this is me with my bestie Abigail, and here's Jen, and this is Marissa," she said. "We are so crazy together. It's hilarious."

This was worse than fucking baby pictures. Don't show me pictures of your friends if they're not either naked, in lingerie, or involved in a sex act.

I met Aubrey at some club when she was bar hopping for a friend's birthday, and I think we made out a little before she had to leave with her crew of twenty. She texted me, and for some reason I answered. She was hot, and while I do enjoy a bar-room public display of horniness with an anonymous girl, this was torture. I could've been spending a lovely evening hate-fucking Vicky who was still attempting to contact me despite having cut her off, but here I was bored and now the girl actually liked me. That's never a good thing. A girl is far more likely to fuck you on the first date in a public place if she isn't really into you. And I didn't want this girl to know where I live.

A tall girl with a bare back and tight jeans walked by, her long dirty blond hair that went to her tight ass and sequined crisscrossing straps were the only things blocking my view of her skin. I kept my eyes on her as she walked to the bar, and met up with a group of girls—all probably models—surrounding a middle aged man in a black suit with a red tie and matching handkerchief hanging out of his breast pocket. He looked to be playing the big pimpin' role, buying rounds of drinks for the long-legged beauties.

She glanced to her right and I could see her face, and immediately knew I recognized her from the time I came on her ass on the balcony of a suite at the Marriott Marquis. It's hard to forget such a romantic moment.

Aubrey continued with her garbly gook, always conscious to avoid making eye contact with me, never losing focus on her texts. "Uh huh," I agreed. "Sure. Of course."

Who cares what the fuck she was saying?

The girl whose ass I came on stood up, and started to walk away. She went to the left of the restaurant, around the bar, through the crowded restaurant, and up the stairs, most likely making a bee-line for the bathroom.

"Look at this picture," Aubrey touched her phone, and shoved it into my face.

"Yeah, I'm really pumped to see more pictures of you and your friends and your awesome lives," I said. "They're just so funny. I just need to use the restroom."

"Okay." She went back to phone functions and eating with her hands as I took off in pursuit of a better life, or at least a better night.

I walked across the restaurant and quickly up the stairs, catching up with her near the top. My eyes fixated on her back and tight ass and the pink thong sticking out of the top of her form-fitting blue designer jeans as I moved behind her into the narrow hallway. I couldn't call out her name, being that I didn't know it, so I casually tapped her shoulder. She turned around holding a purse in her right hand.

"Hi," she said.

"What's up," I said.

"You said you were gonna call me," she said.

"That's just something you say," I replied.

She turned away, and started walking.

"Wait, wait, wait," I said, "I'm just joking."

She turned to me, her perfectly primped brows raised with a cool sense of skepticism.

"Okay, normally, it is something you say," I said. "But in this scenario, my phone was stolen and I lost all my numbers. So I couldn't call you. But, I hoped I'd run into you again so I could steal you away from another one of your boring dates."

"You're an asshole," she said.

"Uh huh."

She opened the door to the ladies' room, and took a step in. I followed. "What are you doing?" she said.

"Well there's a bathroom," I said. "It's not quite a balcony, but it's probably a nice bathroom. And there's a handicap stall, I would assume."

"Do you really think I'm gonna fuck you in the bathroom?"

"Well I don't see why you wouldn't."

"You really are an asshole."

"Is that good or bad?"

She cracked a smile, her lips pouting as her intense eyes looked right through me.

"Both," she said.

"I'm not surprised," I said.

"I'm still not fucking you in the bathroom.

"Do you wanna go to my place?"

"No. I have respect for myself."

"So you didn't have respect for yourself last time?"

"No actually I did. See, I respect myself enough not to fuck somebody who doesn't call me."

"I told you. I lost my phone."

I didn't see what the big deal was. I mean it had only been like six months. I didn't want to come off clingy.

"I'm sure that's what you tell all the girls."

"No, usually I don't care at all what any of the girls think."

"Do you want some blow?" she asked.

"I would love some," I said.

She motioned with her hand toward the handicapped stall.

"I'm not fucking you," she said as she opened the stall door. "We're just doing coke."

"Of course," I said. "We're keeping things innocent."

She pulled a gram of coke from her designer purse, dipped her Barney's card in it putting a bump on the corner. She pushed it under my nose, inviting me to do the honors. I snorted off the corner with my right nostril, feeling the sweet intensity of the blow and the drip into my throat, and then she took her turn.

"Shall we have another?" she said.

"Of course."

"So I saw you're with some hot date," she said, as she prepped the Barney's card. "What are you doing in here?"

"I was thinking you'd save me from a shitty date, like I did once for you."

She blushed, "I would've but you stalked me into the bathroom."

"Well, I couldn't take another second with her."

"Where's she gonna think you are?"

I took a snort, "I don't care."

She did one more bump and tucked her card and blow away in her purse. "Do I have anything," she said, leaning her head back. I looked, wiping some excess yayo from her nose then halted for a second as we looked in each other's eyes. This bathroom moment was romance at its best.

"You're good," I said, then turned my head away. "What about me?"

I leaned my head back and she looked down at my nose. She towered over me in her five inch heels, as she was already my height or a little taller naturally. She dusted my nose off and then kissed me passionately, pushing me back against the stall wall. Blow made her feisty. I reciprocated, kissing her back and slamming her against the other wall, feeling her warm bare back, and squeezing her tight ass. The kissing continued and I yanked her long hair, then pulled her perfect tits out of her skimpy top—there was no bra to slow me down—and firmly squeezed her fake D cups, and sucked on them.

As her breasts were in my mouth I felt her legs gyrating and looked up to see her biting her lip as she closed her eyes. I was getting so hard as I pressed against her. She pushed her crotch hard into me and I dug my fingers down the back of her pants, putting my hand inside her pink thong, pulling on it and feeling her ass. I unbuttoned the front of her jeans, yanking them down and pulling off her thong and sticking my fingers into her warm wet pussy, then putting them in her mouth. She savored the taste of herself.

I grabbed my throbbing erection and slipped right in. I squeezed her ass tightly as I held her against the wall and drove my cock all the way into her warm pussy. She yelled as she slammed her head back, cracking hard against the wall.

There was a tap at the stall door, and an Asian man with a strong accent spoke, "Sir, you could not be in the ladies room."

We didn't respond, I just kept railing her.

"Stop," she mouthed to me.

"I'm not through yet," I mouthed back.

"Stop it," she mouthed.

"Did you come?" I asked as I squeezed her tits, and sucked her left nipple.

"No," she mouthed.

"Well then we can't stop," I mouthed.

There was another sound at the door, this time a light pounding, and the accent continued. "You can't be in girl's bathroom, you must go."

"My girl's throwing up," I said. "I came into see if she was okay. We would appreciate some privacy."

I fucked her pussy hard. "Stop," she mouthed, then put her head back, and opened her mouth wide as I continued thrusting.

"Come on, sir, you must come outta there," the man continued.

"I'll come, I'll come," I said.

"You must go, now," the man said.

"She's yacking, man," I said. "I'm holding her fucking hair,"

"Eeew, this is disgusting," an obnoxiously loud voice that sounded like a Long Island Jewish woman said.

"Get them outta there," another woman's voice said.

"I'm never coming back here again," the Jew voice promised.

Damn, that voice was almost strong enough to make me lose my wood. Luckily the girl was really hot so I proceeded. "What are you doing?" the girl mouthed, her cheeks rising high as she strived to muzzle her laughter. I continued pounding her pussy harder. My breath was heavy, I was panting like a dog as I felt my dick about to explode.

"Ohhh," she screamed out.

"Get outta there, sir," the Asian voice said.

"I... Uh, I, she's very iii-lll," I said as I shot a massive load into her warm pussy. "Ill. Ill. Oh."

"Oh, oh, oh," she screamed out. "Yes!"

"She's all about the vomiting," I said as I rest my head on her shoulder. "She's a model."

"Shut up!" she mouthed, then smiled, struggling to stifle her chuckles.

I let out a sigh, and a couple deep breaths as my cock fell out of her. "You okay honey?" I said, in a normal voice.

"Yeah honey," she said, pulling her thong and jeans up. "Thanks for holding my hair. I'm uh, I think I'm gonna be alright."

She fixed her top, making herself presentable to the outside world.

"What is going on in there, sir?" the Asian voice said.

"Let's go," I said, pulling on my pants.

I opened the stall door, and held it for the lady, following her out to find a tiny Asian man who looked like a younger version of Mr. Miyagi. There was also an angry Asian lady and several prissy bitches looking on in disgust. What kind of a swanky place was this? It's time to worry when people aren't fucking in your bathroom.

"You have to leave," Miyagi said. "You've disrespected my establishment."

"Hey, your sushi and sake made my lady vomit," I said, "disrespecting the temple of her body."

"Get out of my restaurant," he said.

"Relax, we're leaving," I said. "You don't need to use any of the moves you learned in the dojo."

They escorted us through the front and I looked across the restaurant to see Aubrey was still enamored with her phone, and didn't notice. I could have left money with Mr. Miyagi so the check would be paid, but I didn't. Aubrey wanted to text while talking to me, good, she could pay the tab.

As we walked out the door I turned to Miyagi, "Hey... You're no Pat Morita."

When we got into the street she was laughing uncontrollably, bending over and holding her stomach in hysterics. "You alright there?" I said. "You're not really gonna puke are you?"

"Hahahahahahaha," she was squealing. "I just, I just—hahahahaha. You're so wrong."

"We've established that."

We walked down the street arm in arm on the perfect cool and clear October night, ridiculously laughing, my hand on her ass of course. "You could feel free to grab my ass, too," I said.

She squeezed it. "Cute ass," she said.

We went into a pizza place—a grimy little hole in the wall like all the good New York pizza joints—and perused the selection of massive round slices in the case. "Give me two plain, and two pepperoni," she told the chubby Italian man with the Bronx accent.

"What kind of fucking model are you?" I said.

"One who's a pig," she replied.

"I'll have the same," I said.

We both grabbed diet cokes from the case.

"Twenty-five seventy-nine," the man behind the counter said.

I pulled my cash out to pay.

"Oh I got this," she said.

"I'll get it," I grabbed for it.

"Don't worry. It's not my money."

"Well then by all means."

She took care of the check.

"What, did some sugar Daddy give you a credit card?"

"Yep."

"There's perks to being a model."

As we sat at the least sticky table we could find, a high-top in the corner by the window, she ate like she had a tip on a famine, devouring quickly with no regard for her appearance. I'd found a common bond. More than sex or comedy, more than writing or acting, my true passion of passions has always been food.

"So you came in the bathroom, but I didn't?" she said.

"Well, that's because you were distracted," I said.

"How could I not have been?"

"I managed to get off."

"You men have it so easy."

"Credit cards and allowances, I think you women do okay."

"It has its perks. So are you gonna get me off?"

"Oh so that's why you bought my pizza?"

"You got me figured out."

"I require something a little fancier. I'm a high class gigolo."

"Do you want a canoli?"

"I have a better idea."

I led her three blocks to the alley where my Mercedes was parked, and opened the back driver's side door for her to get in. I laid her down on the seat on her back, pulled her jeans off as I dropped to my knees on the floor and yanked her thong off with my teeth. I put my lips on her clit, lightly chewing it, then put my tongue inside her. Her pussy was flowing so much my face was dripping wet, secretions falling from my chin. I came up and kissed her allowing her to taste herself, and she licked her juices off my primped scruff.

I went back down, firing my tongue inside her as she arched her back, screaming in ecstasy. "Oh fuck, fuck, fuck, AHHHHH!"

I lifted my head, "Shut the fuck up. People are gonna think I'm raping you."

She grabbed the back of my head, and shoved it intensely between her legs.

"Oh Oh.. Fuck... Yeah, yeah, yeah... Ohh," she moaned as I continued the cunnilingus.

As her orgasm culminated she was rather complimentary. "That was so good," she said. "Take your fucking pants off."

She dropped to her knees on the right side of the floor, leaned her head down and unbuckled my belt and undid my pants, putting her hands inside my jockey boxer briefs, cradling my balls and pulling my hard dick out. She gave as well as she got, sucking my cock, licking my balls, and swallowing in the backseat, pulling every drop she could muster like she was a hooker and my cock was shooting hundred dollar bills.

"Fuck you're good," I said. "Thanks for not making a mess of the car. It's new."

She went to kiss me and was so beautiful that the thought of pulling away, which I normally get during a post-blowjob kiss didn't even cross my mind as I nibbled the lips that were just on my cock.

"I'm definitely gonna call you this time," I told her.

Funeral Creepin'

I wondered if I should be crying, and said as much to my father.

"No, you shouldn't be crying?" he said.

"But, it's a funeral," I replied.

"You don't have to cry, this was for the best," my mom said.

"It seems like someone should be crying. I mean, it's supposed to be a sad affair, but people are talking sports and laughing right next to the casket. It's like 'hey, there's a dead guy, let's talk about golf.'"

I had come back to Scranton for my grandfather's funeral. Passing at eighty-seven wasn't a shock by any means, but sadly, he had a brain tumor and the last year of his life spent in chemo had been no life. So my mother was right. Her father's death was for the best. Still, I didn't know how to act. The way I looked at it, he died a year ago, and I'd already done my grieving before his oxygen officially expired. I've never been one to care what people think, but, I did love my grandfather very much and would never want anybody to think otherwise just because I wasn't hysterically balling my eyes out—or even teary eyed. Still, a few hours at a viewing was one thing, but I was dreading the next day's lengthy funeral procession.

Luckily, somewhere in the sea of unknown relatives who assured me how well they knew me when I was a kid, I was able to find a D-cupped distraction to take me away from the sadness and stress of 'to cry or not to cry.' But now I had another nagging question: to creep or not to creep at a funeral?

Uncomfortable and not knowing how we should behave, my sister Valerie and I shivered outside on the steps of St. Thomas' Church the next morning in order to ensure we were in the last group to enter. There was a parade of cousins, great aunts and uncles who I didn't recognize yet felt a need to exchange the most unpleasant pleasantries.

"I remember when you were a kid, I used to come over," some chubby man with a moustache said. I couldn't say I liked where this was going.

"I took you fishing. We should go fishing again," he said as his gray nose hairs twitched.

"Uh huh," I nodded, thinking that even though I'm a fan of Red Lobster why would anybody possibly want to go fishing?

As this interesting exchange continued the D-cupped damsel walked by in a customary black dress, her flowing dark hair worn straight as it should be. She was five-five or six, long legs, skinny but not too skinny. Her dark eyes seemed to be fixated on me as the parade of relatives talking to me continued.

"We'll get together soon," the relative with the 'stash continued. "You'll come by the house for dinner."

As we dawdled into the cathedral Valerie and I sat in the third to last row, away from our parents who were up front, on the right side. I saw Mom was standing up, looking around. I could tell she saw us when her fake smile turned to a scowl. We knew she wanted us by her side, but also knew that we didn't want to be there.

The mysterious brunette sat four rows up. She turned around, and took a long look toward me, a slight smile on her face as she ran her hand through her hair, then quickly shifted her head as if she was looking for someone. Obviously, she didn't want to make her blatant leering overly obvious.

Sitting in the procession, listening to the priest, and the ridiculous chanting way of speaking, I couldn't help but laugh. "What are you doing?" Valerie asked.

"Nothing," I tried to hold my laughter back, finally quieting myself.

The Priest chanted, *"THROUGH HIM, WITH HIM, IN HIM"*

"Hahahahaha," I burst out giggling like a school girl who ate a special brownie.

"Stop!" Valerie demanded.

"FOREVER AND EVER," the chant continued as another chuckle slipped out. I cleared my throat, and then locked my lips tight, my face scrunched up and turning red as I tried to hold in the intense belly laughs.

"James, stop!" Valerie reiterated.

"It's a coping mechanism," I said. "I'm coping."

I busted out another quick laugh. "Coping," I said, stopping myself.

It was time for the "peace be with you." I thanked God that this was almost over – and I was actually in a proper place to thank him. The endless string of handshakes commenced with the people sitting around my pew. "Peace be with you, peace be with you, peace be with you"—what a lie, I hated these fucking people. I didn't want them to have peace. And who knew if they washed their fucking hands. At the end of the "peace", the busty brunette gazed toward me and we made eye contact.

"Speaking of peace, look at that piece of ass over there," I said to Valerie. "She can't wait to fuck me."

"You are so disgusting," she said. "We're at a funeral."

"So? I'm not dead."

"This is not the time, James. We're in church. This is worse than when you laughed."

"It's a coping mechanism... I told you that," I said as I began to tear up. "I can't help it. I'm coping."

"But you wanna be creepin'," Valerie said. "And at our grandfather's funeral."

"Grandpa would not want us to mourn, he'd want us to move on with our lives and have a good time... And he'd be proud if I fucked her."

"You're going to hell. You can't fuck her at a funeral. What is wrong with you?"

"You're cursing at a funeral. Watch your mouth."

My sister is five years younger, but no matter how old we got, and how long it had been since we saw each other, we picked right back up torturing each other like all siblings do. After all, isn't that what family is all about?

Out of respect to my sister, or a fear that she'd tell my mother, when we arrived at the snowy, rural cemetery, I still hadn't made a move on the brunette. As we listened to the priest say his final words while the casket was lowered into the ground my eyes peered from behind my Dolce and Gabbana sunglasses at the sexy funeral goer. She stood to my right, about twenty yards or so away. "What if this is the girl I'm supposed to be with, the girl I'm supposed to spend the rest of my life with, have children with?" I pleaded with Valerie.

"You hate children," she said.

"Well yeah, but, maybe this is the girl that would make me learn to love them."

"I'm sure it's her," she said, a note of sarcasm in her shrill voice.

"Mom always said one day I'll find the right girl who I'd love so much that I'd wanna change for, and I always thought that was bullshit, but what if it is her?"

"James."

"And because of what you say is appropriate funeral behavior—this is a happy funeral by the way, it's not like a kid died—what if I don't make a move and then I never know if she was the one? Wouldn't that be awful? That's not how I wanna live my life."

"Stop it."

"And who are you to lay down funeral creepin' parameters? Who are you to declare what's appropriate, and what's unacceptable?"

The after party at an Italian restaurant in Jessup seemed more like a soiree at Jay Gatsby's than a post funeral gathering. I was surprised there wasn't a big band orchestra belting out Jazz standards, and a dance floor full of drunks hammered on smuggled booze doing the *Charleston*.

I stood by the bar sipping my vodka tonic when the funeral director, Louie Cataldo, slid in next to me, ordering a drink. "Scotch and Soda," he told the bartender.

I didn't think it was usual for a mortuary scientist to attend the funeral after party, but there he was with his tie loosened drinking hard liquor, and sampling the cashews. He had the look of *La Cosa Nostra* but the lightness and humor of a cartoon character. Too jovial for a middle aged Italian, and too animated and amiable to be a profiteer of death.

"You throw a hell of a funeral," I told him.

"Thank you," he said. "Very nice of you to notice."

"So how's business?"

"Not what it used to be."

"Not enough deaths, huh?" I said. "That's too bad."

"Yeah, hopefully things will pick up," he said.

"I figured with the shitty economy and all you'd have more suicides."

"Yeah I thought it was gonna help, but when somebody offs themself, people aren't too wild about spending on a funeral."

"That's too bad. What about muggings gone wrong?"

"Not in this area."

"You may have to move your business to the 'hood."

"They don't have the money in the 'hood," he said. "I'd have to drop my rates."

"It's a shame people aren't spending on death like they used to," I said.

I sat through dinner and still hadn't made contact with the brunette. My sister and I were at our corner table, devouring a feast of manicotti and chicken parmesan.

"You got sauce all over your face, you pig," Valerie said.

I wiped my mouth with a linen napkin, leaving a big, red, marinara stain on it.

"You are disgusting, James," she said.

"The broad's not at our table, so who the fuck cares," I said.

I scraped up the remnants of linguini from my plate, and slopped the last of the garlic bread into the sauce.

"What if she's related to us?" Valerie said. "We don't know a lot of our relatives."

"Who the fuck cares?" I said. "Love is love."

I watched the brunette get up from her table, and walk over to the bar.

"So you'd still?" Valerie asked.

"Of course," I said. "The law is first cousins can't marry, beyond that you could do all the inter-familial fucking you want."

I stood up.

"You have no respect for anything," Valerie said, and stood up, taking a big gulp of her Vodka Cranberry.

"Worst case scenario I meet a relative, make a friend... We could comfort each other in this awful time... We could remember the good times with Grandpa... And related or not, he would definitely think she was hot."

"Don't you dare go over there," she said.

"I'm going," I said.

"You are such a skeeze! What is wrong with you? I'm telling Mom."

"What are you? Five?"

My idiot sister walked over to my mother, appearing to rant to her while my mother looked toward me, with her forehead clenched. I sipped my drink, and played aloof but Mommy was on her way, my sister in tow.

"James, this is not a fucking whore house," my mother said.

"What?" I said.

"You can't be...you can't be *creepin'* at a funeral," she said. "We're in mourning, okay? My father died. I am now an orphan."

"Mom, I know you're an orphan," I said. "I just...It hurts so much and I feel something drawing me to that girl, and I thought maybe we could help each other through the pain."

"Really?" my mother asked, skeptically. Why was my family always skeptical of me?

"Well," I said, "you know how you always say I'll find a nice girl one day, be done with the pigs, and how it's the greatest thing in the world when you're in love?"

"Yeah."

"I'm thinking... You might be right."

"I'm always right."

"I know," I said. "And maybe this girl, I don't know..."

"Do you believe this shit?" Valerie chimed in. "He's so selfish."

"Go talk to her," Mom said. "But don't be full of yourself."

"Yes Mother."

"Unbelievable," Valerie said. "You bought that crap? Oh he's playing you Mom... Using Grandpa's funeral to get laid."

"Watch your fucking attitude, Valerie," Mom said. "You're so selfish... Jealous that your brother's meeting a nice girl."

"That's right. Don't be jealous, Valerie," I said.

"Well I was Grandpa's favorite," she said. "Every holiday he sat next to me. Every one."

"Uh huh," I said. "I can't talk right now, Valerie. I'm going to find love."

The brunette stood by the bar with a jack and sour in front of her. I walked over, and stood next to her, ordering up another beverage. As I waited for my drink her brown eyes looked toward me, then quickly away as she played with her straw. I'd certainly caught her attention but she was playing it cool.

"How awesome is this funeral?" I said.

"What?" she replied with raised eye brows.

"Are you having a good time?" I asked.

"Well, not particularly."

"Aww that's too bad," I said. "Why not?"

"Because it's a funeral."

"Seriously though, this is a blast," I said. "This is better than a lot of weddings I've been to. It's almost as good as a bar mitzvah."

"You're sick."

"Yeah, but... This is still fun. I can't believe you're not enjoying yourself. Are you a pessimist?"

"No, I'm not a pessimist... This is a funeral. You know, it's not supposed to be a good time."

"If you wanna live your life in negativity I can't help you. I'm James."

"Jackie.

We shook hands. "I see what's going on here," I said.

"What's that?"

"You're really sad."

"Huh?"

"You need consoling," I said. "I think we should take a walk."

"Well... okay."

We picked up our cocktails and I led her out to the cozy foyer. The room was bare except for a couch and coffee table, and I invited her to have a seat.

"I can't believe you're not having a good time," I said.

"I can't believe you are," Jackie replied.

"No, I mean I'm sad but, just trying not to think about it."

"Yeah, I get freaked out at these things."

"You look hot for a girl at a funeral."

"Ditto... You know, for a guy."

"You don't think I'd be a cute girl."

"Actually, if you got rid of the scruff... You probably would be."

"Thanks."

We shared a light laugh, smiling at each other in this fairy tale-like funeral setting, experiencing that pause romantic idealists call "a moment". I kissed her full lips slowly, and as our tongues met she pushed me back against the arm of the couch. The action quickly escalated from sweet, soft and slow to an intense, passionate, cannibalistic style maul. This funeral was becoming even more fun.

"We can't do this?" Jackie said.

"Why?" I asked.

"I mean, not here. People are gonna have to walk out at some point."

"Good call," I said, noticing a tiny coat room out of the corner of my eye. "Follow me to our suite, lady."

"Are you crazy?"

"It depends who you ask. Are you?"

"Well I'm a girl, so yeah."

I pushed her inside the coats, pulling up her black dress and down her boy's shorts. If it had been a thong I could have just slid the crotch to the side which would have been of great assistance in a crammed closet, but no. "Why no thong?" I asked.

"Boys shorts are sexy," she said.

"To who?"

"A lot of guys have told me."

"That's because they were so thrilled they were actually with a girl that they didn't think about the difference."

"Come on," she said.

"Boy's shorts are a waste on this ass," I said, slapping her ass, and grasping her firm right cheek.

She smiled, "I'll have to wear a thong for you."

"Oh, is this going somewhere?"

"I guess we'll see."

She unbuckled my belt and my black Hugo boss pants fell to the ground as she ripped open my black tie and opened the buttons of my shirt, feeling my light chest hair and kissing my pecs. No surprise there, I had been working out to get ready to shoot my TV pilot.

I pulled down the top of her dress to suck her tits. They were round, and perfect aka fake, which I'm always a fan of. I pulled up her dress and put my cock inside her, sucking and fucking and pushing her against the wall. As she leaned her head back a top coat covered her face and when I moved in to kiss her, a couple of hats fell off the top shelf onto us, but I kept powering through.

"Oh god, Fuck," she said.

"Shh, shh," I said.

"Fuck me James, oh."

"Whatever you say, lady."

I continued pounding her, holding her ass and kissing her hard. She bit my lip in the sexy way girls do.

"Ahh, ahh, ahh," I gasped.

And she did so again. "Ahh," I repeated, trying to stay quiet and play it cool while I pushed my long cock up against her cervix, as scarves and more hats fell from the top shelf, onto our heads.

"Oh god," she moaned. "Fuck."

The door opened, exposing my bare ass to the world. I stopped gyrating, my cock still inside her, and still hard, as I tried to disappear behind the row of coats, thinking if I didn't move a muscle or organ nobody would notice. But they'd already made us, or, at least my ass. I was afraid to turn. "JAMES!" I heard in a whispered scream.

Fuck. I turned around, "Hi Mom."

"What the-? You're fucking in the coat room!" Mom said.

"Oh, my manners. This is—"

"Your cousin Jackie!" my Mom yelled, cutting me off.

"You told me to," I said to my mother.

"You're my cousin!?" Jackie said. "Gross!"

"How could you say that?" I said. "She's my soulmate, Mom. We couldn't wait."

My Dad arrived on the scene, laughing hysterically, followed by a group of relatives who didn't seem quite as amused.

"What is your perverted son doing?" my mother's older sister, Cheryl, asked.

"He's not perverted," Mom said.

"He's riding his cuz," some random redneck relative of mine yelled out, obviously excited by the notion.

"Yeah," my Mom said, "but there's a good reason. Just let me figure out what it is."

"James," my Dad said, "why don't you... get out of her?"

"That's a smashing idea, but... Would you all mind giving us some space?"

They looked at me like that was out of the question. "So I could pull my pants up," I said.

They walked back into the restaurant. "Come here, baby," I said to Jackie.

She pushed me away, which I thought was a little rude. "Is something the matter?" I asked.

"Eeew, you're my cousin," she whined in anger, her face looking like she just yacked and was trying to get the last bit of vomit out of her mouth. Obviously my spirit was broken, but I forged ahead.

"So?" I said. "We didn't come yet."

"This is gross," she said.

"Wait, *did* I make you come?" I asked.

"You're disgusting."

"Don't get your granny panties in a bunch."

She pulled her underwear up, pulled down her dress, found a stray heel, and tucked her breasts back in. "They're boy's shorts," she said.

"What... Don't get dressed. It's a disservice to both of us to go halfway. I don't like to do things half assed. That's not how I was raised."

She scoffed at this.

"My grandfather always preached 'finish what you start'," I continued. "They left us alone for a reason."

She grabbed her purse and coat and began to run through the foyer, confirming my suspicion, "You must have already came then."

I followed her into the parking lot as she scurried toward her car. Her black three-inch heels hung to the sides of her feet, as she tried to wedge them on. "Did all this mean nothing to you, the way we connected, and consoled each other?" I asked. "This is the start of something good."

"No it's not!" she exclaimed.

"So we have this great time together, a real connection, immense passion, and you find out we're related and you just wanna forget about it?"

"Yeah... And the fact that you don't is really disturbing."

"I'm a romantic, okay?" I said.

"You're crazy."

"Yeah, but you said you were crazy, too. I guess you lied."

"Get the fuck away from me," she said.

"Hey I'm wearing my heart on my sleeve here. And I kinda think it's hot that we're related."

"Yuck," she grimaced.

"Think about it, it's sexy, adventurous, dangerous... Fucking your cousin, doesn't it feel like a wet dream?"

"In fuckin' Kentucky maybe."

"We knew the stakes goin in?" I said.

"What?"

"We knew this was a possibility."

"No we didn't."

"It's a funeral... Why do you think we didn't go into backstories of our lives?"

"Because we were horny."

"Well that's part of it," I said. "But I mean we really rushed into it. Neither of us wanted to believe that we could be related."

She didn't respond, just pulled her keys out and hit the button to unlock her red Jetta. "Are you regretting this," I asked, as she got into the car. "What? Couldn't I at least get your number?"

"Seek help."

She sped out of the parking lot, making a wide left. A forest green Jeep Cherokee Limited honked its horn as it swerved to the right, narrowly missing her. The Jetta revved and she sped away. I began to laugh and lit a cigarette, realizing how much I love funerals.

Louie, the friendly neighborhood mortician, was kind enough to join me outside. He had a big smile plastered across his wrinkled face, his slightly chubby cheeks glowing. "Good work."

"Thank you," I said.

"Cousin or not, she's gorgeous."

"I know, right? That's all that should matter. I could see if I fucked Cousin Sue with the gap teeth or Aunt Terri with the black teeth, that'd be mildly frowned upon, but I fucked a higher class of relative."

"Piss and vinegar, kid. You're full of piss and vinegar."

"Hey though, thank you for everything. This is the best funeral I've ever been to."

"That means a lot," he said.

"I hope you'll do mine."

"I'd be honored."

"Thanks," I said. "It almost makes me want to die.

I noticed my mother walk out of the restaurant.

"On that note, I see my mother's coming to yell at me. Good meeting you."

As I puffed my Marlboro in the corner of the parking lot I saw Mama, Papa, and Sister making a beeline toward me. "Louie, the funeral director is such a good guy," I told them. "He was really more like a Maitre d' than a mortician."

"Good work, numb nuts," my Dad said, in the dry, sarcastic way he spoke. "At least your mother made it *seem* okay though."

"What did you say?" I asked.

"Nothing," Mom said.

"She told them that you were consoling her, she threw herself at you, and you knew it was wrong but couldn't bring yourself to say no," Valerie said, chuckling.

"That's exactly what happened," I said.

"That's right," Mom said. "My mother used to call you Don Juan the Gigolo. And you were only five."

"I can't believe they bought it," Valerie said.

"You really couldn't keep it in your pants, James?" Mom said.

"You raised me to share," I said. "And because of you all rudely intruding on us, she left … And we didn't finish."

"Too much information," Valerie said.

"This is not a laughing matter," Mom said.

"Come on, it's funny as hell," I replied.

"It is hilarious," my Dad said.

"Shut up, Jim!" Mom said to my Dad. "James, I don't even care that it's your cousin… Couldn't you have at least done her in the car?"

"I wanted to take my own car," I said. "You said we had to drive together. You had the keys, and if I asked if I could have the keys you would've interrogated me. And I didn't wanna lie to you, and if I said I was gonna do her in the car, you would not have allowed it. This is really your fault."

"My fault?"

"I told you Mom," Valerie said. "I told you… It was all a scheme."

"Shut up, Valerie," Mom said.

"I'm just saying," Valerie said.

My mother looked toward the ground, rubbing her eyes, shedding a tear as she fumbled with her lighter to spark a cigar, one of those cheap *Middleton's Black and Mild Mild's* with the white plastic filter.

"Hey Mom," I said.

"Yeah," she said, blowing a puff of smoke.

"Do you think Grandpa would be proud?"

My mother took another puff, and then cracked a smile, "Definitely."

Quiet Sometimes Equals Dirty

Although I've always been an advocate of safe sex, sometimes not having a condom pays off.

As a rule I store three condoms inside an Orbit gum pack—a safe and inconspicuous way to carry my bags—but sometimes even a high class player forgets. We're certainly not immune to civilian mistakes; what sets us apart is our innate ability to capitalize on adversity.

As it turned out, my grandfather's funeral coincided with the annual St. Patty's Parade Day so I decided to stick around for the week and slum it up at some of the local joints.

I greeted the girl as I walked up the stairs at 7:30 a.m. at Tink's on the morning of the annual St. Patty's Parade Day. I chatted her up as my friends kept walking on like they often did, and kissed her to get the day's first makeout out of the way. Bridget was a cute little Irish girl with dark brown hair and striking sea blue eyes I couldn't get enough of. Tits, ass, I like it all, but I've always been an eye guy.

We slammed penny drafts at the grimy, multi-level band venue, and her friends looked on in shock as we made out in the packed warehouse style club, kissing and pulling at each other's sweaty hair. They acted like it was the first time they saw a barroom public display of horniness. Other than a minor dry hump, though, she barely went for my cock. Rude, I know, but I let it slide because it was still before 8 a.m. She seemed the wholesome type and attended Marywood

University, a Catholic college known for lesbians and sexually uptight women.

I called her and left a message a few days later when my friends and I were doing Tuesday Wing Night at Mickey Gannon's, an Irish Pub in the Green Ridge section of Scranton. I didn't expect a call back since I figured she'd come to her senses and think that she would be better served spending her time with a more academic type like herself, rather than a charming Lothario like me. How dare I doubt myself?

I was in the middle of a plate of wings when I got a call back from Bridget saying she would be there a little bit later. As we wrapped up eating she showed up with a friend in tow. The majority of my crew cleared out, but my partner in crime, Sean—although sleep deprived and ready to pass out—stayed to fulfill his duties as dedicated wingman and also driver, since he had picked me up.

Bridget's buddy, Kristen, was cute in a plain girl sort of way. She wasn't the usual bombshell that I drag to a bathroom stall, but she seemed cool. She had a physics midterm the next day and had a study guide with her that she perused while we sipped beers and downed shots. I'd give her credit for multitasking but she avoided the drink.

"Bridget," I said, "you're a very well put together girl. I bet you come from a wealthy family."

"I'm not the wealthy one," she said. "Kristen is."

"Really, Kristen ... Rich hmm?" I said. "Do you have a money bin? And if you do have a money bin, do you swim in the money bin?"

Bridget laughed.

"No," Kristen said. "No money bin."

"Really?" I asked. "I thought everybody rich had a money bin. Didn't you, Bridget?

"Ugh, I really ... I really wouldn't know," Bridget said.

"I mean, what rich person doesn't have a money bin?" I asked. "Where do you swim?"

"In the pool," Kristen said.

"You have a pool, but no money bin?"

"Where do you get this money bin BS?" Sean chimed in.

"*Ducktales*...Duh."

"*Ducktales*?" Kristen said.

"You remember *Ducktales*," I said. "When we were kids And Scrooge McDuck would swim in his money bin. How could you be rich and not have a money bin?"

"I don't know," Kristen said. "My Dad's not a duck, either."

Kristen continued to not drink, but Bridget, Sean and I downed shots of Jack and sipped Miller Light. As we stood by the bar to cash out, Bridget had her arms draped around me, her head slightly bobbing. Although we'd only had a few beers and a couple shots she definitely had a good buzz on.

"Here," I said, pulling out cash.

"I got it," the rich one said.

"No ... Come on. We dragged you out on a school night. I got it," I mildly insisted.

"No," Kristen said. "It's cool."

"She's got it," Bridget said.

"Are you serious?" I said.

"Yeah, thanks," Sean said.

"And you say you don't have a money bin," I said to Kristen. "Girls who are cute and pay—now this is the kind of treatment I expect."

Bridget hugged me, and rested her head on my chest. She looked up at me, "If you like Kristen, I understand."

"Why would you think I like Kristen?"

"Well she has money, and I don't."

"So you think I'm some kind of gold-digger?" Which I am, but to call attention to it was just plain rude.

"No," Bridget said, "but you were talking to her a lot."

"Yeah, so she wouldn't feel left out," I said. "You dragged her here, study guide in hand, and she doesn't know anybody. I just wanted to make sure she was enjoying the accommodations."

"Oh that's so nice," Bridget said.

"So you still like me?" I asked.

Bridget kissed me, "I'm enjoying the accommodations."

"So what do you wanna do now?" I asked.

"Why don't you come to our apartment?" Bridget asked.

"Sean's driving, so could your friend entertain him?"

"I think so," Bridget said.

"He'll help her study. He's a good teacher. So we'll follow you."

"Cool."

Sean and I jumped in his souped-up black Volkswagen Golf and followed the ladies back to their palace. It was nice and spacious for a college girl's apartment with hardwood floors and actual furniture, but despite Kristen's well-to-do family, there was no money bin.

We walked inside, and everybody gathered in the living room. Bridget walked toward the bathroom, and I followed. I stood outside the door, acting like I was texting.

"So where's the money bin?" I asked Bridget through the bathroom door.

She giggled. "I'll be right out," she said with a slur.

As Sean and Kristen sat on the couch, she was going through her study guide. Sean, however, was a zombie. He was a professional driver, chauffeuring the well-to-do around in their sedans and Escalades, and his schedule had him awake going on two days. So Kristen, the diligent student that she was, continued to quiz herself.

"I apologize," Sean said, "but I haven't slept. Just keep doing what you're doing, and every once in a while you'll hear me say ... 'Hmm,' 'ohh,' or 'that's cool.' I'm gonna rest my eyes now."

"Okay," Kristen said.

As Bridget walked out of the bathroom, closing the door most of the way, I grabbed her and kissed her. I held her hips tight as I kissed her passionately and then slid my hands to her fantastic ass. It had a little size, but it was good size. As I continued mauling her, I pushed her back into the bathroom.

We sucked face against the wall, knocking into the medicine cabinets as nail polishes, band-aids, and facial cleansers fell to the floor. I unbuttoned Bridget's tight jeans and abruptly pulled them down. Dropping to my knees, I grabbed her ass and got her green thong in my mouth. I bit down and began to pull the fabric with my teeth as I fiercely threw her to the ground, putting her on her back with her head positioned under the toilet bowl.

Don't worry, I was protective.

Her pussy was sweet with a well maintained landing strip, and I ate that hot, wet snatch using my tongue, lips, teeth and fingers. As my mouth was bound tight to her clitoris, I reached up and felt her tits, which were average-sized but perky.

I did my favorite pussy-meal move, squeezing her ass tight as I continued to eat both appetizers, preparing for dinner and dessert. She was coming so much it was like a water main had broken, flooding the building. Thank God there was no money bin to worry about.

"Oh ... Oh ... Oh ... James ... Oh James! God!" she yelled.

"Damn, your cunt tastes like a Clementine Orange," I said.

"Let's-let's," she stammered, smacking her lips. "Let's go in the bedroom."

"Okay."

Still making out, we stumbled into her bedroom, fell onto the bed, and proceeded to maul each other like dirty zoo animals. She unzipped my pants, rubbed my cock as it firmly rose above the waist band of my standard black boxer briefs, and used her teeth to bite the elastic and pull my underwear down and off. I figured I'd earned this treatment with my sensual bathroom oral rape.

Those blue eyes looking up at me were so sexy as she licked both sides of the hard-eight. First she played with my cock and licked it, never rushing, and then once my wanker had made its way into her mouth, she eased her face onto it. She sucked cock with the rhythm of an R&B legend, first slow and sensual, then speeding up the pace, and her eyes always fixated on my face.

I wondered where she'd learned her skills. This broad must have had quite the whorish past. I love when it's the girls you'd least expect. Could she finish strong, though?

She sped up, sucking with the passion of a movie star in the last five minutes of a formulaic rom-com, but this performance wasn't getting a PG-13 rating.

"I'm almost, I'm almost, I'm almost," I said as my eyes were crossed, and mouth agape. "Okay ... I'm just about ... there."

I remained in suspense over the question of "Will she swallow?"

Without hesitation, she guzzled my cum like a frat boy funneling cans of Keystone Light. She took in her protein like a body builder, then licked up the sides, dabbing the tip of my cock until the orgasm was complete. I was left with my usual post-come moronic smile and goofy laugh. Ah, the after-effects of a blowjob. That quiet Academic sucked cock like a barroom whore. Although, I wasn't surprised because a player can bring the pornstar out of a nun.

She lay next to me on top of the covers, staring at me with those gorgeous blue eyes as she wrapped her arms around me.

"You like what I did when you came out of the bathroom?" I said.

"You surprised me," Bridget said.

"What'd you think I was gonna do ... Bake you a pie?"

"I thought you were gonna kiss me."

"I did."

"I know."

"Should I have acted differently?"

"No way."

"You like how I pushed you into the bathroom?"

"Yeah."

"That was the plan."

"Was it?"

"Yep," I said. "Get you away from everyone so I could have my way with you."

"Good plan."

We hugged for a few minutes then started slowly kissing again. I went back to playing with her wet pussy, fingering and licking.

"You wanna fuck me?" I said.

"Yeah," she replied.

"Give me a second."

I scurried out of the room wearing just my black boxer briefs, my cock at full mast, and rushed into the living room. Sean's head rest flat against the back of the couch while he closed his eyes. Kristen was still by his side, still hard at work studying her Physics. She looked up from her study guide.

"Hi," I said. "Pay no attention."

Kristen had a big grin on her face. Girls like the way I look in my underwear and she was trying to play it cool, but I could tell she was casually glancing at my covered cock.

"You couldn't put your pants on?" Sean said.

"Couldn't find them," I said. "And anyway, the tip is sensitive."

"Could you have at least gotten rid of the hard-on?" Sean asked.

"Also no. Sean," I motioned my hand for him to come toward me. He rose from the couch and joined me across the room.

"Do you have any... condoms?" I said.

"No," he said, throwing his arms up. "I don't."

"Do you think there's any in the car?"

"No. I'm pretty sure there isn't."

"Fuck ... It'll be okay."

Sean sat back down on the couch, once again laying his head back atop the cushion, and closing his eyes while I broke for the bedroom, now at half-mast.

I entered the bedroom to find Bridget laying on the bed, naked and excited, her fingers in her pussy, her expression already ecstatic. She was obviously ready to feel my cock inside her, and I hated to crush that dream.

"So," I said. "Sean didn't have any condoms."

"Shit," she said.

"I know."

There was an awkward silence in the room, but I got creative. "You know, there are ways to engage in intercourse without the possibility of ... repercussions."

"Eeww," she said. "No... Only if I was, like, with somebody for years."

"Okay... It's just an idea."

"Not a good one," she said.

"Okay," I said, "when there's a problem you have to think outside the box."

"No... I like it in the box."

"Alright... So come here."

"What?"

"Just come here," I said.

"Okay."

She slowly moved toward me putting her hand on my chest, and kissing me, then halted. "Stay away from my ass."

"Chill ... Nothing's going in your ass."

"That's right."

Bridget lay in my arms. I kissed her, and she again put her hand on my erect wang. As she rubbed over my boxer briefs, I grabbed her ass tight.

"No ass," she said.

"I know... So you don't want me to grab it?"

"You could grab it."

She put her right hand back into my underwear, again playing with my cock.

How was this gonna play out? Was she on the pill, was I getting the ass, or was I getting head again? I was rooting for BJ number-two because nothing beats a BJ.

When you're in high school or your late teens and you're getting blowjobs all the time, it's like 'when am I gonna get laid already?' It's a big thing for a girl to give it up. But once you get into your early to mid-twenties the girls have had sex a few more times and they're like, "Wow, this is good. I'm not sucking anybody's dick. Fuck me!"

The past few years I'd been lucky enough to have a string of women who felt empowered with a dick in their mouth, but I still remembered the days when lays were easy but blowjobs were much more difficult to manifest.

I lay back and watched as Bridget again dabbed my dick tip with her tongue, looking up at me with those gorgeous blue eyes. And down she went. A second blowjob. Wow, I really had misjudged this girl. What a pleasant surprise. Two blowjobs in an hour—now that's a good fucking night.

"Oh... Yeah," I said in ecstasy. "God. Suck that cock, bitch. Suck that cock, bitch! Suck that fucking cock!"

She increased her pace, bobbing and weaving like a prize fighter making an eighth round attack. She wasn't just relying on her right, she was using both hands, firing smooth combinations. Bridget went all the way up and down the solid shaft, tasting every inch of my balls like she was licking the batter out of a bowl her mother made brownies in. As I watched her pick up speed I was ready bust.

"Oh, oh, oh yeah, you suck so good," I exclaimed as I my cock boiled over, firing an abundant amount of hot cum into her mouth.

She swallowed my load whole before coming up for air again. I wondered how she did it without an oxygen tank.

"Well my friend's really tired, and you've got class in the morning, right?" I said afterward.

"Yeah," Bridget said. "Eight a.m."

"Cool," I said. "Well we better get going. Have a good night."

No condoms, two blowjobs, I felt like I was being rewarded for screwing up.

The Girl Next Whore 3

It was a long drive back to New York from Scranton so I gave Noelle a call on the way.

"Hey, whore," I said.

"I'm no one's whore," she said.

"I didn't mean it like that."

"Sometimes I don't know what you mean by the things you say, James. I feel like you believe you're your persona, and you lose who you really are."

"What are you talking about? That's what you like about me."

"Why did you call me whore?"

"You told me to."

"Well, that's not who I am."

"You said you wanted to be my whore."

"Goodnight, James."

"I called you what you want to be called."

"No girl wants to be called a whore. It's degrading."

"I thought that's what you liked about it!"

"Good night."

"Noelle, come on, Noelle, I didn't mean it."

I looked at my phone and saw she'd already hung up. Fuck that. She was my fuck buddy, I was treating her like she asked to be treated. No way was I putting up with this shit.

A few days later after a show at some dive bar, somewhere in the country upstate, I sat in the driver's seat of my Benz getting a hummer from a girl who sat in the front row.

"Oh Noelle, Oh," I yelled out.

The broad pulled her mouth off my dick.

"Who the fuck is Noelle?!"

"It's uh, that song, "Noel, Noel"," I said. "I got my first blowjob around Christmas time, in my mother's car, and that was the song on the radio so sometimes I, uh, sing it when I'm getting sucked. Sorry."

"That's hot," she said.

"Uh huh."

"Well keep singing," she said.

"Yeah, I'll do that."

She went back to sucking and I continued the caroling.

"Oh, Noel, Noel, Noo---elle.. Oh Noelle... Oh. No. Elle."

Those were the only lyrics I knew so I had to make do.

"Why don't you call me whore?" she said.

"Okay, I gotta go," I said, pulling my pants on and throwing her out of the car.

Okay, that didn't happen... the putting my pants on, I mean. I'm just using a little artistic license. If this had been a PG-13 rom-com, I'd have gotten out of the car and run straight to Noelle, but this was a real-life adventure with a fan, and I had an image to protect. That involved blowing my load in her mouth, on her face, and on her tits. She should have just swallowed it whole because she left my Benz sticky. I let her finish blowing me, calling her whore as I climaxed in her mouth and further imagining Noelle.

So after I sent the adoring fan back to the guy she came with, I texted Noelle.

"Hey Noelle," I wrote.

(Notice I didn't say whore.)

"Hey!" she responded. *"You wanna come over?"*

"I'm out of town tonight," I replied.

"How about tomorrow?" she asked.

"What time?"

"How's 8:30?"

"See you then."

I had a chance at redemption, to prove to her that I could have sex without being degrading to women. I'd have to undo everything I learned watching porn.

Noelle didn't mention the convo from a few nights earlier and I figured I'd best shut the fuck up and screw, I mean, have intercourse.

I've always heard broads—I'm sorry, *women*—complain of guys who just lay there without saying anything. I'd have to become one of those guys. I'd have to start wearing khakis and crocs to the bar, and get a job as an engineer.

We fucked missionary style, and I just looked in her eyes and we kissed. I was careful not to move too much, or go too hard—she might see that as degrading. I felt like I was in high school, fucking in my bedroom while my parents were home and trying to be as quiet as possible so we got off without getting caught.

This was what she wanted: politically correct sex, or as I like to call it, boring lazy intercourse. My rhythm was slow and peaceful, and not a single obscenity came out of my mouth.

"Am I your dirty little whore?" she yelled out.

"Uh, no," I said. "Absolutely not."

I continued my powerless gyrations, careful only to caress her ass and breasts gently—no squeezing, slapping or swatting would be tolerated.

"Why not Daddy?" she said. "Why not?"

What was I supposed to say?

"Call me a whore, call me a whore!" she said.

I guess that was my answer.

"You're a... Whore," I said nervously. "You're my fucking whore."

Uh oh ... I hoped the cursing wasn't too much.

"Slap my ass! Pull my hair! Come on, dammit, hurt me! I'm a bad girl and I need to be spanked."

"Okay."

I tapped her doupa in the most playful manner, careful not to exhibit any force or cause any part of her buttocks to redden.

"I said slap my ass... Don't be a little bitch!"

I couldn't win with this chick.

"Okay," I said.

"Harder," she said.

I struck her bottom with a bit more intensity.

"I said harder!" she demanded.

What was going on? Was I gonna make her come and then have her yell at me for my language?

It was like I was fucking Jekyll *and* Hyde. At this point I guessed my girl next whore was back to—well I don't know if you could call it *normal*, but back to being my kinda broad. I slapped her ass hard and loud, which just made her increasingly animalistic.

"I'm fucking you, you whore! I'm fucking the shit outta you. Are you Daddy's little whore? Are you Daddy's little whore?"

"You're hurting me Daddy! You're hurting me!"

"You want me to stop?"

"No fucking way, Daddy! Hurt me, hurt me, hurt my cunt with your big fat cock! Fuck me, James! Fuck me! I'm nothing but a whore! I'm nothing but a fucking whore!"

I swatted her tight beautiful ass harder, and harder. She needed to be punished.

"Damn right you are! You fucking whore! You little slut! Your tight fucking cunt feels so good! Fuck ... Oh fuck yeah, bitch!"

I pulled her hair, yanking her head back, making her tighten and contort. I was gonna get screamed at when Dr. Jekyll overtook her body, but fuck it. I was fucking my whore.

"Where do you want it, whore? Where do you want me to come?"

I asked for her preference to show how giving I could be.

"All over my face," she said.

"Well then I better pull out."

I was on my knees in front of her face, jerking my cock.

"Jerk it Daddy! Rub that big cock for your little whore."

"Anything for my whore."

"Blind me with your cum, baby! Shoot it all over! Shoot it all over!"

I blasted my load all over her face, as she closed her eyes and leaned back like she was bathing in a warm shower. Noelle licked at my cum and rubbed it in with her hand, sucking what was left off her fingers.

"Oh yeah Daddy," she said. "That's good … It's warm and smooth and tasty."

"I'd like to bottle and sell it, but I haven't found the right manufacturer."

Surprisingly, through multiple texting encounters and a few phone calls and several fucks, Noelle offered no more criticism of my degrading language and behavior. Good. She was my whore, I was her daddy. That's the way it's supposed to be with consenting adults.

Luring a Bisexual Broad

I could see that my sister was wondering why my date was groping her. It might have helped her to know that I was using her to lure a bisexual girl.

It began a few weeks earlier when a chemically enhanced bleach-blonde stripper and I were vibing as we sat in the corner of a steamy gentleman's club with just the right amount of sleaze to make you want to be there. I did that thing where I look a stripper in the eye and in doing so make her forget she's wearing a G-string while dollar bills hang out of her garter. It's just an innocent exchange like she'd have if she were a business woman, in full clothes and heels that didn't turn her into a power forward.

We bonded over her new boobs—stellar D-Cups—the same way I would've with any broad who took pride in her recent enhancements. Implants are meant to be a conversation piece, at least for the first year. As I was grabbing them, and offering positive feedback, Phoenix mentioned that she was bisexual.

"Really?" I said. "I wouldn't have expected that in a stripper, I'm sorry, exotic dancer."

"Honey, I don't do it for the art, I do it for the money," she said. "I'm a stripper."

That was hot, and she was making no effort to get money out of me.

She found me on Facebook with a profile under her real name, Jordan, and we began to talk frequently. However, once she saw my sister Valerie's pics, she constantly inquired about her. So I decided my Penelope Cruz-replica of a sister, who doesn't roll that way, had a better chance of closing this broad than I did.

At first I was jealous, but then I came up with a plan: invite her to hang out with us, get close to her, get rid of my sister and go for a complimentary private dance. Maybe we'd even pick up another girl together or call one of her stripper friends. You know, to make the evening a little more special. I was thinking of the lady's needs, not my own And her boobs were big enough to go around.

So I proposed the idea of hanging out and of course she asked if Valerie would be there. "Certainly," I replied.

"Is one of your whores really coming out with us?" Valerie asked when I proposed a night out.

"How dare you call her that," I said. "She's a close friend."

"She's probably some stripper or pornstar or something."

I didn't say anything.

"She is, isn't she James?"

"I... I don't know what she does."

"Yeah right."

"You know I only talk about me," I said. "I don't care what other people do."

"That's true," Valerie said.

My sister was wrought with nerves as the bisexual beauty's socially acceptable dance moves quickly escalated to poetic gyration. She was working my sister as if she was a drooling paying customer. Valerie quickly escaped Marquee's dance floor and cornered me by the bar.

"Your friend totally wants me," she said. "She's trying to get in my pants!"

"What... Are you crazy?" I said.

"James, she's all over me," she said.

"Oh come on," I said. "That's how you dance."

"I know when I'm wanted," Valerie said.

"Are you that delusional?" I said. "You are so vain. You think everyone likes you. Where do you get off making these false accusations? That's how rumors get started. You should be ashamed of yourself!"

I figured I'd put up enough of a fight to convince Valerie I had no idea that Jordan was attempting to engage in any lewd and lascivious acts with her, so I wouldn't be getting a call from my mother. Now I had an opening, and it was time for me to casually use it.

"Just in case, why don't you take off," I said, pulling out a twenty. "Here's money for a cab."

"I thought you said she doesn't like me," Valerie said.

"Well, this is just a precaution on account of you being so desirable."

"I am desirable."

"Of course you are."

Valerie left the meatpacking district club leaving me to explain the situation to the stripper who had her heart set on ravaging my little sis. It wasn't easy to break the news, but I did my best.

"My sister had to leave suddenly," I said. "Her stomach was bothering her. She apologized."

"Is she okay?" Jordan asked. "Maybe we should go."

"No!" I said. "She'll be fine. Her wishes are that we stay here, and bring sexy back in her honor."

The stripper was now giving me the explicit attention she had intended for Valerie. She needed to channel her pent-up sexual urges somewhere, and I was there. And who looks more like my sister than me?

She grinded into me hard, working me like a stripper pole, rubbing her straddled thighs above my knee, while pushing her pelvis against my hard-on. She bit my lower lip, pulling on it, then shoved her tongue in my mouth as the strobe lights created a dizzying effect.

"Do you wanna bring sexy back some place else?" she said.

"I don't see why not," I said.

Since Valerie was crashing at my apartment and I knew I couldn't compete with her, we went to Jordan's apartment, which had a delightful crack house ambiance to it. Still, she insisted I take my shoes off.

Jordan came out of the bathroom in a green bra and thong, with garters and matching stilettos, walked to the iPod dock on the nightstand, and put on "Pornstar Dancing". She moved to the stripper anthem in front of me, swaying her body and rubbing her crotch and new boobs. She moved closer, putting her knee between my legs and grazing it against my crotch. I was already at half-mast.

She rubbed her crotch against mine, lightly gyrating as she put her arm on my shoulder, blowing in my ear and then nibbling the lobe, and sticking her tongue in my ear. Her hot breath and saliva took me back to the first time I got a lapdance on my eighteenth birthday, making my cock fully hard. She turned around, bending her knees as she pushed her ass back and forth in front of me, and bouncing her ass cheeks with the utmost muscle control. She pushed her ass into my crotch, rubbing slowly back and forth on my hard-on.

She moved her ass off me, looking back toward me as she slapped it.

She took off her bra, slinging it over my shoulder, and put my face between her perfect tits, squeezing my cheeks with her tits. "It's a shame your sister couldn't join us," she said.

"I know," I said, my words muffled as my face emerged from her rack. I looked up at Jordan. "She really would have had fun."

Jordan looked down with a devious smile then straddled me, dry humping me hard, demanding I suck her tits.

"Squeeze them, suck them, oh yeah, oh," she said.

She humped me hard as I squeezed her ass. I turned her on her back and pulled her thong down with my teeth, her green stilettos still on and up in the air and underwear halfway down as I shoved my head between her legs. My cheek rubbed against her light brown landing strip as she pulled the thong off over the eight inch heels.

I sucked her clit and squeezed her ass cheeks, then put my tongue inside her. As I ate her intensely, she had her hand on the back of my head, grinding her long red nails into the back of my neck, pushing me further into her dewy twat.

"Eat my pussy, eat my pussy, oooh uh," she squealed.

She moved to all fours on the bed, her ass in the air as I fucked her doggystyle, while firmly grasping her hips. I rest my hand on her long serpent tramp stamp as I fucked her hard.

"Oh Valerie, fuck me with that big black strap on you dirty bitch," she said.

I pondered this, slowing my pace.

"Is that a compliment?" I said.

"Harder, Valerie," she said. "Fuck me harder!"

"Of course."

I pounded her harder with my cock, which she apparently saw as a big black strap on.

"Oh, oh, fuck me Valerie," she said. "You ate my cunt so good."

"It takes a woman to know a woman," I said.

I can't wait to eat that pussy of yours," she said.

"I'll let her know."

As promised I delivered the message to Valerie and although flattered, Valerie didn't follow up. I thought that was a little rude, but not my business.

The Soccer Mom

I stood on the sideline at my friend's son's soccer game, tweeting about how bored I was, when I felt a tap on my shoulder. "What are you doing here?" I heard from a woman's voice so sexy it could only have become that way through years of cigarette smoke.

I looked up to see sex—well, a soccer Mom that looked like sex anyway. The first thing I noticed were her massive fake tits because she was about six-foot tall, and wearing four or five-inch heels and a tube top that had them on display like it was the front window of Bergdorf's. They weren't your usual D or double-D tits, these were easily Es or Fs. I looked up to see her bleach blonde hair and a tanned face masked by oversized designer sunglasses.

"I was trying to bet on the game but apparently they don't keep score," I said.

"You look great," she told me as she lightly touched my chest with her long dark pink nails, running her fingers over my torso and grazing my belt buckle. If there was an international signal for "*I want to fuck you,*" this was it.

"Thanks babe. You too," I said. "I like the outfit. It's very event appropriate."

"Just because these bitches are frumpy old whores, doesn't mean I have to be."

"I agree," I said. "I think it's great that you're six-foot tall and wear five-inch heels to a kid's soccer game. That's class right there."

"Thanks sexy," she said. "You wanna go for a walk?

"How do you know her?" Eric whispered in my ear.

I shrugged my shoulders because I didn't know or care. Whoever she thought I was, it couldn't be any more difficult to pull off that role than it had been to pretend to be a lawyer. We walked away leaving Eric to enjoy the intense athletic competition. "Where ya going?" he said.

As we sat in her black Range Rover I licked the tops of her massive fake tits , above her pink lace bra while I squeezed them. I took her bra off, wedging as much of her massive right tit as I could into my mouth, and sucked her nipple.

"Don't forget the left," she said, as she rubbed it.

I sucked her left tit as I squeezed her hips before my hands made their way to her amazing ass.

"Remember when you did blow off my tits in the bathroom at The Willow?" she said.

"Of course," I said.

Now I actually did remember her.

"I really wanted to fuck you that night," she said. "You were such a good kisser, and your dick was so big and hard."

"Uh huh," I said. "First off thank you... But, why didn't we fuck? The Willow's got a great bathroom."

"I was there with my boyfriend, silly."

"Oh that's right."

I mauled her, pressing her head against the window as I kissed her, sucking on her collagen injected lips. I pulled her hair, putting my tongue in her ear as her legs quivered.

"Oh fuck yeah, James. Oh," she moaned, letting out a squeal like she was already on the verge of making a mess.

"You're wet aren't you?" I said.

She smiled mischievously, biting her lip as she salivated, her legs gyrating as if she was humping the driver's seat. I put my hand on her crotch and could feel she'd soaked through her jeans. I undid her belt yanking down her tight pants, and started to rub the front of her pink lace thong.

"So you felt my big cock at The Willow?"

"Yeah."

"Does size matter for you?"

"Oh god yeah. I like a big fucking cock."

She rubbed my hard shaft over the denim, and I undid my belt, and pulled my jeans and boxer briefs halfway down. I then grabbed her and pulled her onto my lap.

"Put it in, sexy, put your big cock in me. Oh fuck me!" she screamed as she straddled me.

I reached down and pulled a condom out of my jeans.

"What the fuck you doing? I have my tubes tied," she said.

I threw down the condom and slipped my cock into her soaked pussy. "Get up here soccer Mom, you fucking whore!" I demanded as I fucked her raw-dog.

"Yes I am James. I'm a dirty fucking whore. That's why I need such a big cock in my filthy pussy... Ohhhh... Ohhh... James," she panted.

I yanked her hair hard as she rode me at full speed, her massive breasts bouncing in my face while her head slammed against the ceiling. I grasped her hips tight, pushing her back and forth as I sucked on her perfect tits. "Fuck me James, fuck me hard James," she moaned. "Oh god I like that cock. I like that big fucking cock in my filthy pussy!"

I slapped my hands onto her ass, intensely grabbing it as I drove my cock further inside her. "Ohhhh... I'm coming! I'm coming! Oh!" she screamed out as her cum shot against my cock.

I kept pushing hard, and began to intensely pull her hair with both hands. She yanked the back of my hair then pulled my head into her tits.

"You like my big tits? You like my big fucking tits?"

"They're fucking amazing," I mumbled against her rack.

"My boyfriend paid for them and you're the one sucking on them."

"Well tell him thank you. It's nice of him to loan them out."

"FUCK ME!"

She grinded her long pointy nails into my back and rode me hard as I pushed my cock deeper inside her warm cunt. I pulled all the way back, then slammed it up inside vigorously, and spanked her ass.

"People are walking by," she said.

"Do you want me to stop?" I said.

"Fuck no!

"Good call."

"Spank my ass!" she said. "Spank my tight ass! HARDER! HARDER! You like that ass? Spank my ass, spank my ass... I said HARDER!"

I spanked her so hard the palm of my hand had gone numb with pain.

"Oh yeah, yeah, yeah."

Her pussy gripped me tight. She whipped her head back as she came hard all over my thrusting cock. I slammed her pussy hard as I yanked her long hair, pulling her back and forth.

"This is what you get whore," I said. "This is what you get for being a fucking whore!"

"OHH ... OHHH ... OHHHHHH ... Oh god, oh god, James! Fuck me!"

"Oh yeah...Oh yeah... Oh... Fuck yeah. I'm coming. Oh yeah."

She bounced hard up and down as I fired my load into her. And I kept thrusting.

"You want more, you filthy cum slut?" I asked in a commanding voice.

"No, no, no," she said. "Oh God."

With my hands grasping her tight ass I pushed her to the left, laying her down across the shifter, her head jammed against the driver's seat door. I pushed my cock into her as I pulled her hair with my left, and put my right on her throat. I yanked her head and choked her simultaneously as I fucked as fast and powerful as I ever had.

"Yeah, fuck me!" she said. "Oh yeah!"

"I'm gonna come," I said. "I'm gonna come... Oh."

I shot another massive load into her pussy, and she made a gulping noise as she came simultaneously.

"AHHHH AHHHH AHHH J-J- JAMES! AHHH!"

"Oh god," I said. "Oh Jesus. I'm coming, I'm coming, I'm coming. Yeah, yeah, yeah that's a good pussy."

I let her throat go and she kissed me, mauling me with her tongue, slobbering all over me.

"That, oh my God... I never came so much, or so hard, or," she said as she caught her breath, and lit a cigarette. "Oh baby. Nobody, nobody ever fucked me like that before."

"Don't forget to tell your boyfriend that," I replied. "In fact, I should really send him a thank you note for letting me use his tits."

The Girl Next Whore 4

Noelle was at my door with two grocery bags full of containers of several different kinds of sushi. She had all my favorites—spicy shrimp, shrimp tempura, lobster roll, and dancing roll.

"Do you have any soy sauce?" she asked.

"I'm pretty sure I have the low salt one," I said.

She put the bags down on the counter, and I pulled the soy sauce out of the cupboard and grabbed a couple plates.

"How was your date?" I asked.

"You tell me," she said, pulling the sushi containers out of the bag and setting them on the counter. I started to open one.

"No, no, no," she covered the container with her hand. "You eat after we fuck."

"I'm really hungry though."

"Don't take that tone with me."

"Fine," I said. "But only one round... Then I eat."

I held her from behind on my bed, my arms around her caressing her breasts as I pulled her into my chest, thrusting into her pussy slowly and sensually as I softly kissed her collarbone. I rubbed my hands across her ass cheeks as my cock was inside her, kissing the side of her neck. She peaked over her shoulder at me, looking at my eyes like they were a plasma TV and it was *Shark Week*.

She kissed me with a subtle passion, and we savored each other's tongues as she reached down between her legs and fondled my balls. I rubbed the palm of my hand down her stomach, across her belly button and used my fingers to put pressure on her clit.

"Oh James," she said quietly.

I kissed her lips again. Her eyes didn't leave mine even though I was behind her.

She lay on her back on the bed and I held her tight as I pushed deep inside her, our eyes locked on each other, my throbbing cock on the brink of boundless jubilation. Our fucking had gone from a metal song to a power ballad and I fucking liked it. There was something warm and soothing about it, like drinking cocoa next to a fire on a cold winter day.

She got on top of me, easing her way onto my big, hard cock, and leaned forward feeling my chest and kissing me, then cuddling my head with her arms as her tits pressed against my face. She pressed her chest against mine, her eyes staring at me as she sensually glided back and forth on my cock.

"I wanna feel your cum inside me," she whispered.

She kissed me deep, sucking on my lips, and putting her tongue in my mouth as she continued riding me.

"Baby," I said. "Oh."

"James," she said. "Oh James."

"I'm gonna come," I said.

"Oh, oh, oh," she said as she threw her head back, arching her body and putting her arms behind her, gripping my thighs for balance. Her tits bounced as her eyes closed and body pulsated. I held her ass tightly, spreading open her cheeks while we shared both a smile, and long, simultaneous, orgasm.

She leaned forward, kissing me slowly then resting her head on my chest as we lay in each other's arms reflecting on the earth shattering bliss I just provided. I sat up on the left side of the bed, and lit a cigarette. I took a drag then put my smoke in her mouth and she blew a puff.

"I like the way your leg tenses up at that last moment," I said, "and then your ass does like a stutter step into me."

She blushed, putting her head to the side, looking away from me as her face became flush.

"You're blushing," I said.

"No," she said.

"What?" I said, placing my cigarette in the ash tray on the nightstand. "Look toward me."

She turned her head back in my direction, pulling the brown pillow over her face.

"It's bright in here," she said from beneath the pillow.

"Not as bright as your face," I said.

I grabbed the fluffy pillow, trying to pull it from her face, and she yanked it back, further burying herself, as I continued trying to wrestle it away. I pinned her down on her back, holding her arms and kissed her slowly enjoying the softness of her lips and the warmth of her tongue.

"So I have a date tomorrow night," she said.

"Cool," I said. "So what's this dope buying me for dinner?"

"He's not a dope."

"Oh."

"No. So I'm really nervous."

"Why's that?

"Well, I haven't been on a first date in a while."

"You go on dates all the time ... And then fuck me and feed me after."

"Well, this guy's different."

"How's that?"

"Well he went to high school with me, and I had a crush on him then. And he recently friended me on Facebook and we've been talking every day...And...I don't know."

"Okay."

"So I have a question for you."

"Okay."

"Well... We were supposed to go out to dinner, and then he didn't call me. But he texted me the next day and acted like it never happened. Why'd he do that?"

Whoa whoa whoa ... This wasn't the supportive whore who gratified my ego. This was not why I let her call me Daddy while I blew my load in her face. I was just her fuck buddy, and now she wanted me to be her Wingman? I contemplated this for a few seconds but she asked again.

"Why is he doing that?"

"Ugh."

"Is he not into me?" she asked.

"Um ... No," I said. "He ... He definitely likes you, but..."

I knew we were supposed to be "no strings attached," and I'm The Wingman, but giving her advice about another guy she wants to fuck was making my stomach turn and dick shrivel up. However I somehow mustered the strength to offer legit advice.

"He's playing it cool," I said, "and not showing too much interest, because it'll make you like him more."

"Why would it make me like him more?" she inquired.

I paused. "You wouldn't be asking me about it if it wasn't."

"But … Why is he doing it? Why can't he just keep the plans?"

"Don't you play guys all the time?"

"Uh huh."

"He's been played before. He knows the game. So he's going on the offensive. Otherwise, you'd be playing him."

"He probably doesn't like me."

"No, he does."

"Why though?"

"You're a beautiful girl next door with an amazing smile and great eyes who's hot, beautiful and cute all at once. You're smart, sweet, hilarious…And you fuck like a pornstar—but he doesn't know that. Does he know that?"

"This is our first date James," she said.

"That doesn't mean shit," I said. "I like to fuck at least five times before a first date. I take things slow."

She laughed, smiled and blushed all at once.

"You say the sweetest things," she said as her beautiful skin turned rosy red and eyes lit up as if I'd just gotten down on one knee in front of the Christmas tree at Rockefeller's Center.

"Well, you just made me feel better," she said.

"Thanks," I said.

"Okay if I make you feel better in return?

"What are you gonna do?"

She started to blow me, licking my cock up and down, then came up for air.

"Thanks for the advice," she said.

"Sure thing," I gave her a 'thumbs up' as I looked down at her face inches above my boner.

She continued to suck my dick as I lay back in nervous disgust. Biting my lip and twitching at the idea of these sweet lips on another cock, I nearly lost my wood. I was stressed about the situation and needed to talk it over with someone—but that someone was usually Noelle. If I consulted any of my friends they'd just call me a pussy for getting attached to my fuck buddy. And, I couldn't really talk about it with any of my other broads.

As she was leaving Noelle was kind enough to reassure me that should it work out, she would still keep me as a fuck buddy. Normally I'd be fine with that—turned on by it in fact—but this was eating at me. Yet, I kept quiet—which is hard for someone who never shuts up.

After she bounced I was lying in bed, this date of hers pissing me off as I ate the leftover sushi that she had brought me. I banged my fist against the headboard, the wall and the nightstand and pounded my chest in disgust. I have a tendency to punch things when I get upset, but it usually has to do with my career. It had been a while since I'd punched anything over a girl.

I needed a therapy session to help me with my feelings for my fuck buddy so I worked it out over afternoon anal with Sandy, my trusted sex therapist. "Fuck my ass, James, fuck it hard," she said.

"I am, I am," I said. "So what's the deal?"

"She likes you a lot, but she doesn't think you like her."

"Why not though?"

"You're pretty intimidating to a lot of girls,"

"Is it because my cock is huge?"

"No."

"Is my cock not as big as I thought?"

"No, it's a great cock, James, magnificent."

"Well thanks for clearing that up."

"Okay," she said, "you could go a little harder."

"Sure," I said. "Sorry I was distracted."

"Oh, fuck, yeah," she said. "You see James, ohhh, it's where your cock has been."

"So does she like me?"

"Babe, she loves you, but girls are more afraid of getting H-U-R-T than anything, so she'll go out with losers from high school to avoid that. You said yourself, she told you from the beginning she was a woman scorned."

"What should I do?"

"Keep your guard up, kid. She loves you. But it takes a crazy bitch to know a crazy bitch, and she's a crazy bitch."

"That is true. You are one crazy bitch."

"I know," she said. "Could you choke me now please?"

"Sure."

The Girl Next Whore 5

I had to help the girl I'm fucking garner a man's attention. I was her wingman.

We were going to a party at her friend's house, and now it was my job to help Noelle use her pussy power to land my competition. I felt like a baseball player on Arnold Rothstein's payroll.

Most house parties consist of a bunch of dudes in their thirties, a beer pong table, and video games. That's not really my scene. However, this was the rare house party that was actually one I would normally want to attend.

We were on the Upper East Side by the park on a Saturday night in an opulent brownstone with leather couches, a full bar, and a catering staff. Despite the prevalence of hot, wealthy ass, expensive finger foods, and most likely good coke, I wasn't in the mood. At this point my only aim was to appear as a wingman, while actually being a cockblocker.

"That's him over there," Noelle told me. "What do you think?"

I didn't say anything, because if I did, it would've been to bash his pedestrian appearance and yuppie demeanor. He stood by the bar drinking an imported beer and breaking down the specifics of why it was eighteen dollars a bottle. He was one of those guys who was around my age but was already acting and appearing middle-aged. He probably had been since high school. Being that

I'm past the age that I need someone older to buy my beer, I have no use for people like that.

"So what do we do?" Noelle asked me. "Like, make out?"

"No, no, no," I said. "You gotta be subtle."

"Okay," she said. "You're the master."

"Fucking right I am. See, he's looking over. Don't look."

"Should I go talk to him?"

"Fuck no."

"Well ... why not?"

"You're here with me. You let him come to you."

"What if he doesn't?"

"He will."

"How do you know?"

"Why wouldn't he?"

"Well... I'm here with another guy. What if he gets turned off?"

"Right...That's what always happens. Someone we like is doing somebody else and we don't want them anymore."

"I see your point," she said. "But do you really think this will work?"

"You're so beautiful, you could be here with me, covered in Herpes sores, and he'd still want to fuck you."

"You made me blush again."

We smiled for a moment. And then I caught myself.

"All right," I said. "I'm gonna make myself scarce. You hang here, sip your drink, and let him come to you."

I walked away, mingled with some of her awful friends, and helped myself to a stellar spread of hors d'oeuvres. As Noelle hung out in the living room talking with her girlfriends, my competition finally approached. It made me want to spit up my cheese and crackers. As she stood across the room flirting with the asshole—he was nowhere near as pretty as me—I stood by the house's full bar drinking a sugar-free red bull and vodka, which I followed up with a couple shots of Jack. There were sexy girls all around but I didn't feel like fucking any of them ... Unless, of course, Noelle was also involved.

I walked on to the back terrace to have a cigarette, only to find Noelle lip-locking her prized mark. *Fuck.* His back was to me and she stood against the railing and looked over his shoulder in my direction. I hid my frustrations with a slight nod and turned around, and walked inside. I played it cool in her presence, but inside I was fuming.

I moved through the dining room as conversations about charity balls, Hampton parties and politics encompassed the room.

"Hey... you're the comedian, right? The Wingman," a girl I'd normally want to bend over stopped me.

"Yeah, I heard you were coming," she said. "I was at one of your shows, and you were so funny. You were making fun of my boyfriend and hitting on me ... you know, part of the show. He and I aren't together anymore. Wanna do a shot?"

"I have to pee," I said, and kept walking. I was in no mood for pleasantries.

She turned around, raising her voice in disgust. "What? Do you think your shit don't stink or something?"

"I just have to pee," I replied.

I couldn't believe that I was smitten with Noelle. Why would anybody want to go and ruin a perfect situation like ours by falling for the person? Quite frankly, it was masochistic. I was fucked. But I'd accomplished my mission; I'd gotten her hooked up. I wished I wasn't such a good wingman.

I went into the bathroom, a lavish marble one with a massive luxury shower cabin, and toilet with a bidet like you would expect. I stood at the sink, and washed my face, slowly rubbing the cold water against my eyes. I turned the faucet off and looked up a bit at the mirror to see my eyes red, and skin flush with anger. I stood all the way up, fixed my collar and took a deep breath. Then, I launched into a temper tantrum like a preschool kid who'd been watching *The Sopranos*.

"FUCK, FUCK, FUCK!" I said to myself. "COCKSUCKER PRICK DOUCHEBAG ... I'LL KILL THAT FUCKING CUNT MOTHERFUCKER!"

I made a fist and reared back to hit the counter, but restrained myself from damaging the elegant lavatory. Instead, I behaved like a grown-up and channeled my anger elsewhere. I belted myself in the right temple. BAM...BAM...BAM...Three times.

"OWWW!"

My head felt like it was going to explode. I rubbed it but couldn't find the goose egg. I splashed some more water on my face, adjusted my hair—which was still perfect, just like Warren Zevon sang—stretched my neck and rejoined the soiree. I walked down the stairs and found Noelle and the prized pony by the kitchen table, snacking on cheese and crackers and remnants of shrimp cocktail.

"Could we talk?" I whispered to her.

"Sure," she said, taking a bite of her Triscuit. "Kevin, this is my friend James."

"Hey," I said.

"Nice to meet you," he said.

"James is a comedian," Noelle said.

"Cool," he said.

"Yeah you gotta go see him," she said. "He's got a TV pilot being pitched to HBO, Showtime, FX."

"That's great," he said. "What's it called?"

"It's called *The Wingman*," I said.

He laughed.

"It's about a professional Wingman," I said. "He's paid to help people get laid."

"That's cool," he said. "I'd like to come out and see your stand-up sometime. I love comedy. You got anything coming up in the city?"

"Yeah, actually. I have my show running at Broadway Comedy Club."

"Okay," Kevin said. "What do you think, Noelle? Would you go with me?"

"Yes," she said. "It'll be a good time."

"That'd be wonderful if you guys came," I said. "Noelle, could I talk to you for a second?"

"Sure," she said. "Excuse me."

"Nice meeting you Kevin."

"You, too."

We walked upstairs to the hallway, where we stood by the bathroom I just came from.

"So you like him, hmm?" I said.

"Yeah," she said. "He's cool.

"Is this because I denied your request to lick my ass?"

She chuckled. She had the cutest laugh, every time I heard it reminded me of the first time a hot girl at a comedy club laughed at one of my jokes.

"Come on, James," she said. "You weren't into me like that."

"It wasn't you," I said. "I'm just not into having my ass licked. When I was a kid my mom found skid marks in my underwear, and it always stuck with me."

Again, she let out that beautiful laugh.

"You're gone all the time," she said.

"I gotta work," I said.

"Well, you're getting laid all the time."

"Well ... That's what made me good at it."

"Yeah, it did."

We stared at each other with deep intensity as she stood there in her little black dress and fuck-me pumps. Her eyelashes were flawless, her smile wide and natural, and her hair flowed gracefully past her shoulders.

I moved in to kiss her, and our lips locked. It was a perfect moment where the mauling was mutual. The soundtrack went from power ballad to a dirty rock n' roll song in the span of seconds as I pushed her into the bathroom, and she jumped up on me like so many times before, wrapping her firm thighs around me as I propped her up against the wall. I stuck my hand under her dress, and her legs squeezed me tight as she pushed her pussy against me. I felt her crotch with my right hand and found that she was already leaking on the floor. It was like she'd left her lingerie out to dry, and there was a rainstorm.

"We're gonna leave a mess," I said, as I kissed her, sucking on her lip.

"I want you so bad, James," she screamed out.

"I want you, too, baby."

I often use "baby" because I often forget girls' names, but not with Noelle.

"Ohh...ohh...ohh...yeah!" she cried out, as I kissed her and felt her clit from outside her black lace thong.

I barely touched her and she was already getting off.

"You're gonna need a change of clothes," I said, as I pulled down her thong and jammed two fingers into her pussy.

"Yeah, yeah, yeah, ohhh!" she squealed. "Fuck me, fuck me!"

I made it three fingers. She held onto me with her left hand and used her right to undo my belt. I helped, pulling it off as she violently pushed my black pants down and massaged my rock-hard cock.

My pants were around my ankles. I was wearing my healed Italian creepin' shoes, so this was going to be a test of balance. Luckily, Noelle had already gotten off and I was on the verge so I wouldn't have to stay upright too long. She reached down and grabbed my cock, quickly inserting it into her warm pussy.

"Oh ... oh ... ohhh," she said, as if about to cry tears of ecstasy. "Oh James, fuck me!"

It felt so good as the tip slid in. It was tight and wet, and she started to ride me like she was giving my cock an exorcism. I held her up and thrust my hips back and forth, slamming her moderately so I could hold it together longer.

"Harder, harder," Noelle said. "Fuck me harder, James!"

She yanked the back of my hair, and I gyrated harder as her pussy grew tighter. I ripped down the top of her dress and adjusted her black bra to suck on her magnificent rack. "That's right," Noelle said. "Suck my tits, suck my tits."

I thrust harder.

"Oh god James!" she said. "Oh god .... Yeah ... Fuck me ... Fuck me ... Fuck me!"

I slammed her as hard as I could.

"Oww!" she screamed out.

"Oh god," I said. "I'm coming, I'm coming... You're so fucking hot! So fucking hot, you whore!"

"God, I'm your whore, James," she said. "I'm your whore. Oh your cock is so good ... Ohh. Give it to me, Daddy!"

I blew a prodigious load into her toasty twat so hard that had my dick not been inside her it probably would've squirted five feet in the air. It only made her crazier, so I kept going, slamming hard to keep my dick up. She was practically convulsing.

"Yeah Daddy," she said. "Yeah, yeah, yeah."

"Oh god," I said.

I could feel her coming.

"Again," I said. "That's awesome."

I pounded her pussy as she came again, clenching so tightly that I couldn't hold my cock in her; it pushed me right out.

"Oh god, your cum feels so good James. So good."

She dropped to her knees and licked my dick.

"Ahhh...ahhh...ahh," I gasped. "Careful, careful, careful... I just came."

She licked my dick up and down, sucking on my balls, then stood up. I held her against the wall, her head resting on my shoulder, as I firmly grasped her hips and looked into her eyes. She was blushing from pleasure as she attempted to catch her breath.

"Oh James... You fuck me so good, baby," she said, letting out a sigh.

"You're so fucking beautiful," I told her.

We casually walked out of the bathroom, our clothes tattered and hair disheveled, like celebrities leaving an LA club on TMZ. We walked down the stairs to see Kevin in the living room, looking straight up at us but trying not to be obvious.

"Hey," Noelle said to him.

"Hi," he replied. His voice had lost the enthusiasm it had the last time we spoke.

"So good seeing you tonight," she said. "I guess I'll see you soon."

"Sure."

I made my way to Kevin. "It was great meeting you, buddy," I said. "Can't wait to see you at a show."

"Yeah," he said.

He no longer seemed interested which was a little rude, but still, I wanted to make sure he was provided with first-class accommodations. "Facebook me in advance and I'll make sure you're in the front row," I said. "Oh, here's my card."

Kevin just stood there and didn't even thank me, the ungrateful cocksucker. He didn't compliment my card or anything. Even in the megalomaniac culture of *American Psycho* they had the decency to admire each other's business cards.

Noelle and I got into the car and laughed the whole way back to her place. We kissed passionately goodnight and she went inside. We weren't the type to demean beautiful bathroom sex with a sleepover.

I woke up in my bed excited and happy as thoughts of Noelle fluttered through my brain. Something was different. A weight had been lifted from my shoulders as I finally accepted the intense feeling in the pit of my stomach. I just lay in bed and thought about her as I cuddled my pillow and smiled. I wasn't even thinking about sex; I was thinking about how much fun it had been just doing nothing together. I sent her a text before I lit the day's first cigarette, or drank the day's first Diet Coke.

"How you feeling today babe?"

I looked at my phone, constantly checking it all day long, but she didn't write back. I texted two more times, but nothing. The next day I called and left a message. I saw she was on Facebook chat and tried to make contact. No response.

It was Thursday night, the night she usually went to the Galway Hooker in the West Village for Happy Hour. I found her at a table with her friends eating a massive pile of Chicken Nachos and drinking tall glasses of beer at a table by the window.

"Hi," I said.

"What's up?" Noelle said.

Her less attractive friend, Renee, who she rarely hung out with, chimed in. Slightly chunky, sort of plain, somewhat busted—Renee was probably the top crop on her minor league team, but now she'd been called up to the big leagues and was relegated to bullpen status.

"It's a girls' night," Renee said.

"Really?" I said "If it was a girls' night you'd be home eating ice cream and watching *Sex and the City*, not dressed like you're working for tips."

I meant that comment in the context of the group. Noelle, of course, looked sexy as hell, like the stripper you had to buy a VIP dance from just so she would talk to you. Renee was more the type who would work the room for dollar dances all night.

"So what's up with you?" I said.

"Nothing," Noelle said. "Just busy."

"I can't—I can't hear in here," I said. "Could we go outside a second?"

She hesitated for a moment. "Sure," she said.

Renee looked on with a nasty puss on her un-striking face as we set off through the crowd. We stepped onto the sidewalk, and I led her a few steps away from the door which was inhabited by a group of smokers that was big enough to fill up a bar.

"So...What are we doing?" I said.

"I had some time to think," she said.

Fuck, that couldn't be good. A woman with time to think poses a danger to herself and anyone she comes in contact with. I don't recommend a girl ever engage in independent thought— especially when I'm the subject of her rumination.

But I was feeling like Jerry Maguire—I'm a huge Tom Cruise fan—and I was thinking the girl next whore might "complete me."

"Oh?" I said.

"I just... Don't know who you are."

"What the fuck are you talking about?"

"You get so lost in your character that I don't know you."

"What about when we lay in bed talking and joking? What? That's not the real me?"

"I don't know," she said.

"You know me babe," I said. "The guy who listens to you, and compliments you, and makes you laugh."

"You're a comedian. You make lots of people laugh."

"Well I make you blush, too."

"You make lots of girls blush."

"Well I'm not disputing that, but, none of those girls know me like you do."

"It's just too hard to be with you."

"So because you think I'm hot and I know how to fuck, you won't be with me?"

"Right."

"That's ridiculous."

"I know."

"What the fuck is the problem?"

"I think you're degrading to women."

"You used to like that about me."

"James."

"I treat you very well. What about the great time we had in the bathroom?"

"Bathroom sex is degrading."

"That's what you liked about it."

"In a fuck buddy, yes ... But I can't have a boyfriend who degrades women."

"So you'd rather have a boyfriend who doesn't fuck you right?"

She looked away, toward the busy street, biting her lip, "James."

"I'm just saying, you like to be called 'whore' and have your ass smacked, and call me 'Daddy' while I shoot loads of cum on your face."

"Fuck you!" she said.

"What? I'm just 'saying,' what you call 'degrading' seems to be what gets you off. So, would non-degrading sex really make you come over and over, and over and—"

Noelle cut me off in frustration, raising her voice, and talking angrily with her hands. "I don't know, James! So what? It was fun, and spontaneous, and exciting, and passionate, and romantic, and dirty, and FUCKING AWESOME!"

"Well, thank you," I said.

She pulled back, took a breath, and harnessed her emotions. "But not anything I want in a boyfriend."

"Do you know how ridiculous that sounds?" I said.

"Uh-huh," she said.

"Okay ... So we'll just stick to our original arrangement?"

"Yeah ... That's not gonna work, either."

"And why's that?

"Because," she said.

"Because why?"

"Because," she hesitated, "now I have feelings for you."

"So you can't fuck me, because you like me?"

"Correct."

"And you can't be with me, because you enjoy fucking me."

"Correct."

"Do you have mental problems?"

"I might," she paused. "James, it'll just be too hard."

"Fuck! This happens all the time," I said. "A girl wants to fuck me, then decides she likes me and so is afraid to be with me. What the fuck? I'm sorry you were attracted to me, and I got you off, and made you feel good, and you fell for me.

I raised my voice, "How could I be so fucking rude?"

Noelle did everything she could to hide her smile and hold back her blush, but she couldn't.

She looked at me with tears welling up in her big, round, hazel eyes. I did my best to stay calm.

"Noelle, I want you ... all of you. You're smart, beautiful, funny and you make me feel amazing. I have the most fun in the world doing absolutely nothing with you."

"I'm sorry, James."

I fidgeted nervously. How could she not want to be with me? How could she not want to fuck me? Was she lying? Were the orgasms I gave her not really mind-blowing? Was an eight inch dong not enough for her?

"Is there anything I can do?" I asked. "Just give me a chance."

"I can't," she said. "I need a man who's gonna be the man."

"I am ... That's what I'm telling you."

"You say that now ... but you won't."

"I haven't given you reason to think that. That's something someone says when their boyfriend cheated on them or something. I have shown you the utmost respect.

"Respect? Respect? You refer to me as your whore!"

"You told me to!"

"That was in the beginning. That's not who I am."

"I know that's not who you are. We've been through this. It was what you asked me to call you. If you said call me 'princess' I would have."

"James... Let's not bullshit each other. We had fun. We went as far as we could. Good luck. You have big things ahead of you."

Renee, with her dead eyes and stoic demeanor, walked up and stood next to Noelle, tugging on her arm, "Come on, Noelle."

"I gotta go, James," Noelle said.

"Could you please give us a minute, Renee?"

"No I can't," she said.

"I gotta go," Noelle said.

"Once a player, always a player," Renee said.

"Shut the fuck up," I said.

"Don't tell my friend to shut up," Noelle said.

"Fuck you, asshole," Renee yelled at me.

"Shut up, Renee," I said, then explained myself to Noelle. "She interrupted. This is nobody else's business."

"Don't be mean to my friends," Noelle said.

"That's bullshit!" I said. "I was very nice to Sara... Very! Get a reference from her. Where's she tonight?"

"You called her a whore," Noelle said.

"We were fucking," I said.

"You fucked Sara?" Renee said. "You scumbag! He fucked Sara?!"

"Noelle was there, too," I said. "It was a threesome."

"Go tell the whole world, player!" Noelle said.

"What a scumbag," Renee said.

"I'm not trying to tell the whole world," I said. "I'm trying to have a private conversation with you. But your friends won't allow that!"

"James, I really have to go," Noelle said.

"Well ... Could we get together again?" I asked. "Talk about all this."

"I don't think that's a good idea," Noelle said.

"The answer is no," Renee said.

I shot Renee the type of look a parent gives their kid when they wish they had them aborted, and continued pursuing Noelle.

"Why?" I said. "Because it'll just make you want me more and you'll throw yourself at me and you'll fuck me again, have a blast, get scared and want to get away from me before it gets serious and it hurts even more?"

Noelle stood silent.

"Is that what it is?" I said. "Is that it?"

"Yes, okay!" she said. "Is that what you want to hear? Is that what you want?"

"No," I said. "I just want you."

"I'm fucking sick of this conversation," she said. "Goodbye, James."

"Let me just ask you one thing," I said.

I grasped her hands and pulled her close. Renee stood by with her head shaking, eyes rolling, and mouth snickering. I looked right into Noelle's eyes.

"Do you honestly think any guy could get you off over and over like I could?" I said.

"No."

"So what are you gonna do?"

"Buy extra batteries," Noelle said.

"Huh," Renee snickered.

I shot her another look, then persisted with Noelle.

"And you'll be imagining the bathroom," I said.

"Goodbye, James."

The girls turned around, walking away. "Let's go talk to those hot dudes that bought us that last round," Renee said to her.

Noelle didn't look back, but Renee turned toward me with the most annoying smirk of cuntiness on her face.

"Have fun getting off thinking of me!" I yelled. "Yeah, you love those pictures of my cock, don't you? Fucking huge, right? Think of that when you fuck your little bitch boys!"

A group of old ladies—what my grandfather would have called 'blue hairs', even though he was eighty-five himself at the time—stood idly by on the side walk, cigarettes and Starbucks cups in hand. They looked out of place in the Village, drinking lattes, especially at this hour. It was happy hour and nearly 7:30. They should have been in bed after a long day filled with penny slots in AC, and early bird buffet deals.

"What?" I said. "Do you want to see it?"

There was a dead silence, except for one lady.

"I'd like to," the Old Broad said.

I pulled out my Blackberry and scrolled through my vast portfolio of cock pics. Different angles, looks, levels of hair and hardness, a few costumes—I kept about five-hundred with me at all times. You never know if a girl will want to see one on a cold day, and I'm a grower not a shower.

"Wow!" the Old Broad said. "That's yours? Very nice."

"Thank you," I smiled. "You know I'd throw any of you broads a ride on the bologna pony if it wasn't for the fact that it might kill you."

Now they all looked on, pressing their bifocals against the touch screen, their eyes glued to it like they just saw a UFO. I almost contemplated throwing the Old Broads a quickie.

"I can't believe it didn't work out," her friend said.

The other blue hair's face didn't move, her wrinkles actually tightening up. I hoped she wasn't dead. I didn't wanna get stuck there all night.

"I have a granddaughter who would really like you. Much better than that little trollop and her ugly friend," the Old Broad said, the one who first asked to see my dong.

I doubted that her granddaughter could come close to Noelle, but I figured I could have an uncouth adventure trying. After all, I had to research my next book.

Epilogue

I walked down the street, lit a cigarette, took a drag, and threw my jacket across my shoulder with my right hand, while smoking my cigarette with my left. I couldn't believe I no longer had a girl next whore. My stomach was aching, and my head was starting to hurt as I thought of the times we'd fuck off after fucking—those little things, man, were what I would miss most.

I heard a piano playing, some old school type joint I'd never seen before like Billy Joel would have played before he got big or a wise guy joint Sinatra or Dean Martin would have gathered at, smoking cigars and wooing broads. The place wasn't crowded, by any means, but there were enough people there to make it comfortable without being claustrophobic.

I grabbed a bar stool, and waved over the bartender who was an older guy in a vest, with an earring who resembled my Grandfather, who in turn resembled Robert Conrad.

"I'll have a Vodka Tonic and a shot of Jack," I said.

I quickly slammed my shot, then took a big swig of Vodka as I put my head down, looking at the bar, the floor, and the legs of the exotic women who inhabited this joint. I noticed the different heels, medium to really high in size and price, in an array of colors—red, black, white, gold, blue, pink, leopard and zebra. I picked my head back up and fished the Blue Hair's granddaughter's phone number out of my pocket. I stared at the digits for a moment and then wadded the paper up and tossed it into the wastebasket behind the bar. For all I knew she could be busted. Even though Blue Hair had assured me that her granddaughter was "a peach", I've long since learned that grandmothers do not provide the most unbiased assessments of their granddaughters.

"Another round," I said to the bartender.

He placed another shot glass of jack in front of me, and a rocks glass with my vodka tonic. I took a sip of the vodka and leaned back on my stool. As I took another sip I felt warm breath, and lips against my right ear, and heard a sexy, throaty voice.

"Are you stalking me?" the voice said.

I spun around on my stool. It was the girl from the Balcony and the Backseat and the Bathroom Stall, not in that order though, I believe Bathroom Stall came second. Regardless, from what I could recall she had her own way of remembering me, and I had done nothing to change that perception, so I took another drag and went on the offensive.

"I'm sorry I didn't call you," I said.

"Eh, you are who you are," she said.

"It's nice to meet a girl who knows who I am."

"I do. So, wanna fuck?" she asked.

I looked around and didn't see a Sugar Daddy anywhere. "I don't know. It looks like you're alone, which kind of takes some of the fun out of it," I replied.

This time we ended up in a grandiose bathroom in an ostentatious Park Ave apartment that belonged to her out of town Sugar Daddy. We were in a jacuzzi tub that was big enough for a block key party. But it was just her and I with bubbles covering our bodies, jets in our asses as we passionately fucked and sipped champagne.

"How'd you like to go on a date sometime, like a real one?" I asked.

"Really?" she said.

"Yeah."

"What would it involve?"

"Well, you'd start the evening with me," I said. "And then stay with me throughout the night, not run off and fuck some cocky arrogant gorgeous asshole who rudely flirts with you. So you'd fuck your actual date—me—in the bedroom, backseat or bathroom stall of your choice."

She smiled and kissed me, holding her arms around me tight and nibbling my lower lip. Then looked me in the eye.

"Why don't you fuck me again and then I'll decide?"

THE END

About the Author

James Holeva aka "The Wingman" is an author, comedian, actor and Lothario. He created, starred in and executive produced *The Wingman* TV Pilot which is currently being shopped to networks. He also tours North America with his X-rated, interactive live show "The Wingman Comedy Tour: Comedy That Gets You Laid," and recently recorded his debut comedy album which will be available in 2013.

When Holeva isn't touring, he splits his time between New York City and an array of girl's residences. He also hosts #askwingman Q & A sessions regularly on his controversial Twitter account @wingmanbiz.

Email: wingmanfans@gmail.com

Website: http://wingmanchronicles.wordpress.com/

Facebook: facebook.com/letsgetcreepin